TO CONTROL THEM

DI SAM COBBS
BOOK EIGHT

M A COMLEY

For Paul, my wonderful Financial Advisor, thank you for giving me the idea for this one.

Thank you to Clive, for allowing me to use your fantastic photos for the covers for this series.

ACKNOWLEDGMENTS

Special thanks as always go to @studioenp for their superb cover design expertise.

My heartfelt thanks go to my wonderful editor Emmy, and my proofreaders Joseph and Barbara for spotting all the lingering nits.

Thank you also to my amazing ARC Group who help to keep me sane during this process.

To Mary, gone, but never forgotten. I hope you found the peace you were searching for my dear friend. I miss you each and every day.

ALSO BY M A COMLEY

Evil In Disguise – a novel based on True events

Deadly Act (Hero series novella)

Torn Apart (Hero series #1)

End Result (Hero series #2)

In Plain Sight (Hero Series #3)

Double Jeopardy (Hero Series #4)

Criminal Actions (Hero Series #5)

Regrets Mean Nothing (Hero series #6)

Prowlers (Di Hero Series #7)

Sole Intention (Intention series #1)

Grave Intention (Intention series #2)

Devious Intention (Intention #3)

Cozy mysteries

Murder at the Wedding

Murder at the Hotel

Murder by the Sea

Death on the Coast

Death By Association

Merry Widow (A Lorne Simpkins short story)

It's A Dog's Life (A Lorne Simpkins short story)

A Time To Heal (A Sweet Romance)

A Time For Change (A Sweet Romance)

High Spirits

The Temptation series (Romantic Suspense/New Adult Novellas)

Past Temptation

Lost Temptation

Clever Deception (co-written by Linda S Prather)

Tragic Deception (co-written by Linda S Prather)

Sinful Deception (co-written by Linda S Prather)

PROLOGUE

"*W*hat? Are you locking up again tonight, Mum?"

Tammy tapped her finger on the back of her mobile. "Don't start, Zoe. The boss has other things on his agenda right now; his wife was rushed into hospital, the baby is due within the next few hours. I volunteered to lock up for him, he didn't *force* me to do it."

"Christ, really? You're so naïve, you can't even see how much he takes you for granted, can you?"

"He does not. Let's change the subject. Has Neil told you where he's taking you this weekend? It's all very exciting, isn't it?"

"No, and I wish you'd pack it in doing that. I was in the middle of fighting your corner, and here you are, putting up a brick wall, as usual. Stop it, just stop it. When are you going to call a halt to men walking all over you? You let *him* sodding do it for years, and now that idiot of a boss is doing the very same thing."

"You don't need to look out for me, role reversal doesn't

exist in our relationship. May I remind you, young lady, that I'm fifty, not five."

"Get you. Are you telling me to keep my nose out or telling me it's wrong of me to care about what happens to my own mother?"

Tammy covered the mouthpiece of her phone and let out a sigh. When she didn't answer immediately, Zoe repeated the question, only firmer this time. "Let's not fall out about this, daughter dearest, we've only just started speaking again after a six-month break."

"And whose fault was that?" Zoe snapped.

Tammy was aware that if she didn't back down then there would be hell to pay and yet another strained few months between them. "Mine, dear, all mine, of course." Even though it wasn't. Tammy had tried to offer some unwanted relationship advice for Zoe to take on board about how to handle her fella. Zoe had flipped, told Tammy where to get off, and had great pleasure in pointing out that her mother and father were now the proud owners of divorce papers.

"There, I knew you would see sense, eventually. Now tell that boss of yours to get one of the other staff, preferably a male, to shut up shop at night. It's not your responsibility."

"Ah, now that's a no-no. If women want equality in their roles at work, those words should never leave our mouths."

"Give me a break, Mum. This has nothing to do with equality. I'm talking about basic care for your staff, and you know it. That place takes a lot of money, and the responsibility lies with you to ensure the garage is locked up in the early hours of the morning. That's grossly unfair, especially at your age."

"Jesus Christ, I've heard it all now. If I've told you once, I've told you a gazillion, trillion times, no one will jump me on the way home. If they do, I'd give them what for, without a second's hesitation, you hear me?"

"I do, and believe me, I know what you're capable of when the chips are down."

"Ha, you don't. Your father might, although that's a different story."

"I knew it. You've denied it all these years, but I used to hear you crying in your bedroom at night most of the time. He beat you, didn't he?"

"Yes and no. It was six of one and half a dozen of the other. In the end, I gave as good as I got, no fear about that. Now go and enjoy the rest of your evening. That's an order."

"Okay. Take care. Is your phone charged?"

"Of course it is, or it was. It's running down more every second I remain on the phone to you."

"I can take the hint. I'll drop round and see you tomorrow. It is still your day off, isn't it? Or have you given that up as well?"

Tammy cringed and closed her eyes, not daring to tell her daughter the truth, that it was on the cards if the boss's baby hadn't arrived by the morning. "No, still on a day off. Call round for lunch. I'll fix you a bacon sandwich made in the air fryer, you can't beat it."

"Well, that's sealed the deal. I'll be there with bells on. Love you, Ma."

"Love you, too, sweetheart. Go make wonderful plans for the weekend. You can tell me all about the arrangements tomorrow."

Tammy ended the call as the door opened and one of the regulars came in to pay for his diesel. "All right, Mick, how's it diddling, mate?"

"Hi, Tammy. Same old. The wages don't stretch far enough for the missus to put more clothes in that bulging wardrobe of hers. I fear my dinners are going to get smaller every day until she can afford that new dress she keeps banging on about."

3

They both laughed.

"Go on, give in, you know it'll be worth your while."

"How did I know you'd come down on her side? You women are all the same, you all stick together, even when it's blatantly obvious you're in the wrong."

Tammy gave him an extra-wide grin along with his receipt. "Men, you think you've got us all worked out, but nothing could be further from the truth."

He turned and headed back towards the door. "Ha... have a good one. See you at the weekend."

"I'll be here. Don't forget to bung Sandra an extra tenner here and there, if you want an easy life."

He shook his head and let the door close behind him. Tammy watched him continue to shake his head on his way back to his car across the forecourt.

That's what she loved about her job the most, the banter with the punters. Of course, you always got the miserable bugger swooping in now and again, who did nothing more than give a grunt for a response, but overall, the locals were mostly an agreeable bunch. She left the counter, opened the security door to the till section and carried on stocking the shelves in between serving the customers.

Now and again, she sang along to one of the old tunes on the radio. It whiled away the time, which ultimately meant one thing: the end of her shift growing closer.

There was a steady flow of customers throughout the evening, unusual for a Wednesday night, not that she was complaining. At midnight, she switched off the forecourt lights and called it a day. Then she partially cashed up the till, putting the notes away in the safe and leaving the coinage in the cash register for the boss to deal with in the morning. Fifteen minutes later, she secured the front door and set off on foot. Home was a few streets away. She had walked it many times over the years and never had a problem. A couple of young men staggered towards her, obviously the worse for wear.

"Your mothers are going to hit the roof when they see the state of you, Johnny and Tyron."

"Nah, they'll be tucked up in bed when we roll up. Need an escort do you, Tammy? We won't charge you much for the privilege," Johnny shouted over his shoulder as they passed.

"Cheeky sod. I remember looking out for you when you were wearing short trousers to school."

"I never did. Must be a figment of your imagination, old-timer."

The three of them laughed at the words batted between them. It made Tammy's day, to bring brightness and cheer to everyone she met. Too many of her past years had been stuck in the doldrums. She was glad to see the back of those days, the day her ex had walked out and set up home with his slapper of a girlfriend.

Good luck to them. The cheating fuckers deserve each other after making my life hell. No more. I vowed the day he left that my time would be filled with smiles and laughter and I intend to stick to that pledge.

She turned the next corner, and two more youngsters she knew almost bumped into her.

"All right, Tammy, what are you doing out at this time of night?" Steve asked.

"On my way home to bed, and no, that wasn't an invitation for you to join me," she replied when a devilish grin appeared on his cheeky face.

He thrust a clenched fist to his heart. "Your words cut me like a knife. You spoil all my fun."

"Get away with you. Take care, see you soon."

"You, too, sweetheart."

She carried on walking, the area quiet once more, and was relieved when the back of her house came into view. She preferred to use this way, it was closer than having to go around the front. She shoved open the stiff gate that had warped a little in a recent spell of rain and closed it behind her. The back garden was lit by various solar lights she had installed in the summer. Tammy beamed at the way they lit an inviting path, leading to her back door.

See, Zoe needn't have worried, here I am, home safe and well.

Removing the key from her pocket, she let herself in and put the kettle on.

"I'm dying for a cuppa. It was so busy late on that I forgot to make myself one at eleven, my usual time. Never mind, I'll soon sort that out." A meow sounded in the hallway. "Tigs, where are you? Do you want some dinner?"

Her tortoiseshell cat entered the kitchen and did a figure of eight around her legs. She swooped down and collected her in her arms and snuggled into her fur.

"You smell good. I've missed you so much this evening."

Tigs wriggled free from her arms and travelled back and forth along the worktop, pacing for her food.

"You little minx, I can take a hint." Tammy filled the bowl that had been draining upside down in the sink since break-fast time and placed it on the food mat on the kitchen floor.

Tigs jumped down and tucked into her supper.

Tammy poured herself a mug of tea and went through to the lounge. She switched on the light, stopped mid-step and dropped her mug on the luxury carpet she'd had fitted only the week before. "Who...? What do you want? Why are you in my house? No, don't bother. Get out before I start scream-ing!" Her legs weakened and her heart rate increased.

"Do that and I'll wring your cat's neck," the masked male snarled.

Tammy peered closer to see if there was anything about him she could recognise. There wasn't. His voice sounded disguised. Why? She must know him. Was he a customer at the petrol station?

"Please, don't hurt my poor cat. I'll do anything, just don't hurt her, or me. What do you want?"

"Your money. I hear you have a stash upstairs in your bedroom. You're another one who doesn't like banks, aren't you?"

"Take it. I'll get it for you."

She turned to leave the room, but he launched himself at her and grabbed her arm.

"Stay where you are. No, on second thoughts, get that chair."

He pointed at the single dining chair she kept in the lounge; she had no idea why, it was something her mother had done while she was growing up that had always resonated with her.

"What?"

"You heard me. Bring the chair over here, in the centre of the room."

Tammy walked hesitantly towards the mahogany chair with its Regency-striped padded seat and dragged it into position. Her gaze trained on the man, still trying to work out where she knew him from.

"Sit down," he ordered.

"But... you wanted me to get the money for you." Her voice trailed off when he took two large steps towards her.

Towering over her, he sneered, "Shut that fucking trap of yours and do as you're told, you hear me?"

"Yes. Okay. I'm doing it now." She sank into the chair, her legs easily giving way beneath her.

The man whipped out a length of rope from his jacket pocket and gripped her arms, forcing them behind her back.

"Please, don't hurt me," Tammy whimpered, her mind on

the crest of a wave, ebbing and flowing as she tried to figure out what to do for the best to get out of this situation alive.

Once her hands were secured to the chair, he left the room. The floorboards in her bedroom creaked not long after. She envisaged him ransacking her boudoir in his quest to find her money.

How did he know? What the hell? It's not the sort of thing I tell all and sundry.

She gasped, the realisation dawning on her. The only person she could think capable of doing something so vile was Brian, her ex-husband.

I do vaguely recognise him, despite him trying to disguise himself. Had Brian put one of his friends up to this? Is he truly capable of being this cruel?

The intruder's footsteps thundered down the stairs once more, and he came hurtling through the doorway towards her. "Where's the rest of it?"

Shocked, she vigorously shook her head. "That's all I have, I swear."

"You're a fucking liar."

"I... I'm not. Take it and leave. I don't want the money."

The man produced a long-bladed knife, the tip of which touched her chin, and he angled her head up to look at him. That's when she recognised who it was.

"You? Why? I trusted you. Take the money and go. I promise I won't tell the police."

He laughed. "You won't get the chance." His next movement came swiftly.

The blade felt cold against her throat. Blood gushed from the gaping wound and onto her lap. All she could do was stare down at it seeping into her clothes.

Her life faded within seconds.

CHAPTER 1

*S*am groaned and answered the phone that was vibrating across the bedside table next to her. "DI Sam Cobbs."

"Ah, I've woken you. So sorry to disturb you, ma'am. I'm under strict instructions to contact you and you alone."

Sam switched on the light and noted the time. It was six forty-five. "This better be good."

"There's been a murder, and the pathologist has requested that you, and only you, attend the scene."

"Oh great, sometimes it's such a chore being so popular. You'd better give me the location and a brief rundown of what I'm getting myself into."

"I take it you're going to attend the scene?"

"You assume correctly. How can I possibly turn down an invitation from Des Markham?"

"He told me you wouldn't be able to resist the personal approach." The controller chuckled.

"Did he now? One of these days I'll shove one of his invitations and stick it where the sun fails to shine."

The woman laughed and gave her the coordinates for the location.

"Thanks, I'll be there in around twenty minutes, sooner if I forego my morning shower. It would serve Des right if I showed up smelly."

"I'm sure that would never happen, ma'am. Thank you for agreeing to attend the scene. Drive carefully, it's a wet and windy one out there today. We've already had reports of certain roads being closed due to flooding."

"Thanks for the warning, I suppose it's to be expected at this time of year." Sam ended the call and threw back the quilt, burying her pooch, Sonny, in the process.

He poked his head out from under it to glare at her.

She leaned over and kissed him on the nose. "Good morning. Want to go in the garden?"

He leapt off the bed and ran down the stairs. Sam made a detour to fill the kettle and then let him out into the back garden to do his business. The morning was just announcing its arrival in the distance. She shuddered, the cold suddenly hitting her around the face like an icy slap with a dead fish.

"I'd better wrap up warm today. Come on, Sonny, where are you?"

Her cockapoo joyfully bounded through the back door and sat at her feet, ready to dry his paws on the towel she always kept close to hand. Next on her morning ritual list, she ensured he had a fresh bowl of water down and some food, after which she saw to her own needs, poured herself a mug of coffee and flew back up the stairs to get dressed, knowing that she wouldn't have time to fix herself any breakfast.

Ten minutes later, she was standing at the front door with Sonny's bag of goodies in hand, having already peered through the lounge window to see if there was any sign of life next door. Doreen had been in the process of pulling her curtains and had spotted Sam spying on her and waved. Sam had shown Doreen three fingers, and her neighbour had smiled, understanding the sign language.

"Come on, let's get you settled next door."

Sonny bounced, eager to get on with his exciting day.

"Wish I could be as enthusiastic about my early start. Damn, I forgot to ring Bob."

She searched for her mobile, tucked in her jacket pocket, and dialled her partner's number. His grumpy voice filled the line. "Hey, you should be up by now."

"Are you kidding me? Don't tell me we've got an early one?" He groaned and let out a noisy yawn.

"All right, I won't, but I'd be lying. I'm on my way over there now and I'm requesting your attendance because you know I can't do my job properly if I don't have you by my side."

"Jesus, I've heard it all now. You're such a creep when you're trying to get me out of my pit!"

"I know. Did it work? Are you up yet?"

"Give me the postcode, I'll join you soon. Are you on the road yet?"

"I will be after I've dropped Sonny next door. I didn't even get the chance to walk him this morning. I feel bad about that."

"You shouldn't have a dog, it's not fair on him."

"Did I tell you you're turning into my mother? He's fine, I'll make it up to him when I get home. Doreen will let him have a run in her garden throughout the day. Anyway, that's not your concern, it's mine. See you there ASAP, no slacking."

"As if I would," Bob replied grumpily.

. . .

11

Sᴀᴍ ᴀʀʀɪᴠᴇᴅ at the crime scene on the edge of Workington around twelve minutes later. Des was already suited and booted which made her think he'd been there for a while. Sam removed a new protective suit from her boot, signed the log at the cordon, then dipped under the police tape.

"Ah, nice of you to join us, eventually," Des muttered.

"I got here as soon as was humanly possible. What's your problem, you old grouch?"

"My problem is that someone has tampered with my crime scene, therefore, I'm entitled to be pissed off."

Sam glanced down at the woman lying in the alley. To her trained eye, there didn't seem to be much wrong with the scene. "How can you tell?"

He backed up a couple of paces and folded his arms beside her. "Maybe I said that wrong, I didn't mean messed up as in trampled all over the scene."

Confused, Sam stared at the victim and shook her head. "Will you stop talking in riddles and tell me what the fuck you're on about?"

"The body was moved."

"What? She wasn't killed here?" Sam reassessed the victim and her surroundings. "The lack of blood, that's what you're getting at, isn't it?"

"Yes, there's no doubt there's a fair bit of blood around but not enough for the gaping wound she has to her throat."

Sam's gaze travelled the length of the narrow alley. "The area isn't lit, the alley leads to the back of these houses. Any gates open when you arrived?"

"A couple. One at the top and one halfway down."

"Any sign of a trail of blood?" Sam asked. The area was lit up by a temporary floodlight the pathologist and his team had erected for the occasion.

Des smiled. "I wondered when you would ask that."

"Glad I didn't disappoint. Well?"

"From the house halfway up."

"You knew all along, you were just testing me, to see if I was awake yet, weren't you?"

Des grinned. She swiped him across the top of the arm with her gloved hand and then peered at the sky. "It's started to rain again."

"My boys are trying to get the tent up."

"They're taking their time," she mumbled and glanced over her shoulder at the open gate swinging on its hinges now that the wind had got up. "I'm going to take a look."

"I'll come with you. Just to make sure you don't get up to no good with a possible crime scene."

"As if." At the end of the alley, she spotted Bob's car pull up. She paused and waited for him to join her once he'd got his suit on and signed the log at the cordon. "Morning. In your own time, partner. I'm keen to get on with it."

Bob shrugged. "Don't let me stop you, boss. What's going on?"

"Des reckons the victim has been moved. We're in the process of checking out the surroundings. There are two possibilities. This gate and another one up there were found open."

"Sounds like a plan to me." He searched the ground at his feet. "Too dark at the moment to see if there are any blood trails. Shouldn't we be preserving the scene?"

Sam took a sideways glance at Des. "He's right. Might be worth sticking some evidence stepping plates down before we enter the garden."

Des didn't say anything. He walked away and returned with an armful of plates that he placed leading up to the back door of the property. Sam and Bob picked their way through to the house. They replaced their shoe covers with fresh ones. The back door was ajar. A small cat lingered in the doorway, rubbing itself against the edge of the kitchen cabinet. Des switched on the light, and there, in front of them, was a distinctive trail of blood.

"No question about it, is there?" Sam said, sighing.

"Hard to deny what's before our eyes," Des agreed. "Let's venture on."

He led the way into the hallway and then into the lounge where it was obvious the deadly deed had taken place. "Bingo! There's no doubt in my mind."

"Mine neither. So her throat was cut in here and then the killer moved the body outside. Why? So it would be found sooner?" Sam said, asking the most obvious question that had popped into her head.

"More than likely." Des surveyed the room. "She was tied to the chair, for what reason, that's for your department to find out."

"Possible torture? The killer was after something more than simply taking her life?" Sam replied with two more questions of her own.

"Money, jewellery?" Bob asked.

"Possibly. All right if we go upstairs to have a hunt around, Des? We'll be careful," Sam said, smiling, to combat any objections lingering on his lips.

"If you insist. Make sure you don't move anything, not until my guys have taken the necessary photos."

"I'm experienced enough to know what to do when we get up there. Thanks for the reminder, though."

"No need to be snarky, Sam. You know me, always one to state the obvious when on the job. My aim is always to preserve a crime scene."

"I know, I'm sorry." Sam led the way out of the room and up the stairs.

"You've ticked him off again. When will you learn?" Bob whispered once they were on the landing.

"He's fine, it's you reading things into it. You go left, I'll go right. Scratch that, maybe it would be better if we stick together."

"In other words, you don't trust me."

Sam rolled her eyes. "I wish people would chill out around here." She walked five paces and discovered what she assumed to be the main bedroom. "We'll start in here. Yes, there are a couple of drawers open and the wardrobe doors are slid back. Looks like she stored things neatly in boxes and some of them have been disturbed at the bottom." Sam got down on one knee to take a closer look. Two of the shoeboxes had their lids removed. Upon closer inspection, they appeared to be filled with personal paperwork. She could see what looked to be a birth certificate; maybe it was a death certificate. She kept her promise to Des and didn't touch anything. She stood and moved over to the bed and peered over her shoulder before she opened the drawer of the bedside table.

"He'll swing for you if he finds out," Bob warned, tutting.

"And who is going to tell him? I'm not moving anything, I'm just having a peep, that's all."

A technician appeared in the doorway and shook his head. "I'm going to pretend I haven't seen that."

Sam smiled and closed the drawer again. "You two are spoilsports. Okay, I give up, let's go back downstairs, see what Des has to say about things down there."

They found Des standing in his 'thinker' pose, assessing the chair in the middle of the room.

"A couple of shoeboxes in the bottom of the wardrobe, containing personal paperwork, the usual birth and death certificates, possibly the target to obtain something else, maybe financial, like a bank or building society book," Sam suggested.

"Or cash," Bob threw into the mix.

Sam nodded. "What's your take on things as they stand, Des?"

"Too early to call. The amount of blood surrounding the chair is telling me she lost her life here, or this is where the attack happened, at least."

"She would have bled out swiftly with that severe gash in her throat, wouldn't she?" Sam asked.

"I agree. What I don't understand is the killer's need to move the body. Why would they deem that necessary?"

Sam let out a long breath. "They intended for the vic to be found early. If she lived alone, maybe the killer had a prick of conscience and didn't want her to go undiscovered. We need to find out who she is." She raised a finger and crossed the room to the door.

"Where are you off to?" Des asked.

"There was a crowd gathering in the alley, someone out there must know her."

"Good thinking," Des replied.

"Come on, Bob."

Bob followed Sam out of the house and into the alley. They stripped off their suits, gloves and shoe coverings and dropped them into the black bag next to the cordon.

"You start at that end and we'll meet up in the middle."

"Fair enough. Are you just after her ID?"

"Get her ID and next of kin details, if you can."

Bob set off towards two women who were all smiles the second he began walking in their direction. Sam spoke to a man and a woman in their sixties, their hands locked together.

"Hello there." Sam flashed her warrant card. "I'm DI Sam Cobbs of the Cumbria Constabulary."

"Oh my, we saw her lying there and we're mortified she's dead. She is dead, isn't she?" the woman asked, her voice trembling with emotion.

"Unfortunately, yes, she is. Do you know the victim?"

"Oh yes. She's Tammy Callard," the woman replied.

"And she lives in that house behind us? The one with the gate open?"

"That's correct. Lived there nigh on twenty years, give or take a few years, I suppose. She moved in around the same time as us. This is our house here."

"Did you hear anything untoward either last night or first thing this morning?"

The couple were dressed in their nightwear, matching white towelling robes covering what appeared to be matching pyjamas.

"Can't say we did. The first we heard of this incident was when Roger was putting out the recycling bin. A few of the neighbours were out here by then, and it was Gillian who plucked up the courage to ring the police. She found Tammy… lying there."

"Gillian? Where can I find her?"

The woman jerked her thumb over her right shoulder. "Dyed blonde hair with the short skirt."

"Thanks. Is there anything else you can tell me? Did you see any strangers hanging around, either yesterday or today, or possibly in the past few days?"

"No, nothing out of the ordinary ever happens around here. We usually live in a quiet community. This has come as a severe shock to us, I can tell you, hasn't it, Roger?"

"Yes, Mary, an utter shock. Tammy was such a fun-loving lady. All right, she's been through some unnecessary shit lately, but she was over that and making something of her life."

Sam frowned. "Care to clarify what you mean by that?"

"Recently divorced that cheating scumbag of a husband of hers," Mary was quick to fill in.

"I see. And he left the marital home to her?"

"That's right, moved in with that floozy of his, I believe."

Sam withdrew her notebook and jotted down the information. "Do you have his name?"

"Brian Callard," Roger said. "He's a taxi driver, so he'd have a chance to get here, kill her and skedaddle from the scene quickly, wouldn't he?"

His wife nodded. "He would, and I wouldn't put it past the fucker to do it either."

"I take it the divorce wasn't an amicable one?" Sam asked.

"Far from it. The amount of slanging matches we overheard in the garden at all hours of the day... well, let's just say they were numerous," Mary said.

"Do you know where he lives now?"

The couple shook their heads and shrugged. "No idea. Their daughter would know. Zoe."

Sam's interest kicked up a notch. "Do you have a contact number for the daughter?"

"Sorry, we weren't that close. Gillian will probably be able to give it to you."

"Thanks for your help. I'll be sending uniformed police around later, to take down statements. What number do you live at?"

"Twenty. The gate with the red knocker on it... don't ask," Roger said, rolling his eyes and gesturing with a nod in his wife's direction.

Sam smiled and thanked them for their help, then sought out Gillian who appeared to be shell-shocked. She was sucking on her e-cigarette and staring down the alley at the victim.

Sam was perturbed that the body hadn't been covered yet. "Gillian, mind if I have a quick chat with you?"

"I don't know much. I found her lying here and..." Tears bulged, and one dripped onto her cheek. "How terrible that this should happen, just when she'd started to get her life back on track. Where's the justice in this world, allowing this to happen? Aren't women allowed to be out by themselves these days?"

Sam didn't put her right and tell her that the body had been moved after Tammy had lost her life. "Roger and Mary told me she had a daughter and that you might have a contact number for her, is that right?"

Gillian bashed the side of her head with her clenched fist. "What a dumbo I am. Why didn't I think to ring her? Shock, that's why. I can't think bloody straight, my head's all over the place."

"It's fine, totally understandable. Do you? Have the daughter's number?"

"I'll have to nip home. Do you want to come with me or wait here?"

"I'll come with you, if that's all right?" The rain was starting to come down again, and Sam was eager to keep as dry as possible. There was nothing worse than receiving a good soaking first thing and sitting around in sopping-wet clothes for hours on end.

"Through here. Excuse the mess. My son is supposed to be getting rid of all this crap, taking it to the tip for me, when he finds time in his busy schedule."

"I've seen worse," Sam said, although nothing could be further from the truth. The woman was right, her rear garden was an absolute eyesore and a danger to the neigh-bourhood. Sam tried to hurry the woman, fearing a rat might emerge from the mess and nibble off her toes, given the chance.

"Come in. My address book is in the lounge."

The inside of the house was a stark contrast to what was going on in the garden. "You thought it was going to be like outside, didn't you?"

Sam smiled. "I never assume anything."

"I bet. That mess is genuinely my son's, it has nothing to do with me. He's been storing stuff here for a while, and the weather has damaged it. I warned him what would happen, but he knew best. They always do at that age, don't they?"

"How old is he?"

"Thirty going on sixteen. One day he might become a responsible adult, not sure when that's likely, though. He's got a kiddie on the way, only been with the girl five minutes and... no, I'm not going to get myself worked up about it all over again. It's his life, who am I to interfere in it? The trouble with youngsters these days, is they mess up and expect their parents to get them out of trouble. I had to stand on my own two feet at a very young age, lost my parents within six months of each other when I was only twenty. That was tough, I can tell you. There was no one around to support me back in the day. I just had to get on with it."

"You're right, it's easier for the youngsters today."

"It is, compared to our days. I know that makes me sound ancient. There are so many drama kings and queens around these days. I said I wasn't going to go there so I'll shut up now. Ah, here we are. Zoe Callard, this is her. She lives over in Westfield, not too far. Want me to give you her number and her address?"

"Thanks, that would be a great help." Sam prepared her pen to take down the relevant information. "Wonderful, thanks."

"I know this is probably stating the obvious, but she's going to be devastated when she hears the news. Her mother meant the world to her."

"I'm sure. I don't suppose you know her shift pattern at work, do you? Or where she works? I'm only asking in case I can't get hold of her at home."

"Ah, yes, she works at the local bakery up the road. I think she finishes work at around four, starts at around eight, so you might catch her at home before she heads off."

"You've been a great help. I can't thank you enough. I'll shoot over to her address now, see if she's there."

"Anything to help that poor family out. Tammy was one of my dearest friends. In and out of each other's houses, we were, putting the world to rights over a coffee, several times a week. What the heck am I going to do now without her ear to bend?"

"Sorry for your loss. Losing a good friend is never easy."

"Are you speaking from experience?"

"Not really. Although I did lose someone a few weeks ago... I suppose you could say I used to be close to them."

Gillian frowned. "Sorry, you've lost me."

Sam waved her hand. "Something and nothing, don't worry about it."

"Okay, sorry for your loss, too. I hope you'll remember the good times in the years to come, just like I'll have to. We'd had many of those over the years, especially around Christmas and New Year, you know, the party season. Always blotto, we were. Pissed off our partners big time, that did. Screw them. They both did the bloody dirty on us, sick shits. Gutless sods, couldn't tell us to our faces, we had to find out the hard way. Twats. Oh dear, you have work to be getting on with, you don't want to stand around here, listening to me pull all the bad names I know out of the air."

"You're all right, you're bound to be bitter if someone has been unfaithful to you."

"And the rest, with one of my best friends, too. So I've lost her friendship as well. We made a pact years ago, never to be tempted to do the deed with each other's fella, but she took great pleasure in rubbing my nose in it with that one."

"You're better off without her, without either of them, if that's what they got up to. So sorry to hear that. I'm going to

21

leave now, see if I can catch up with Zoe before the baker's gets busy. Thanks again for all your help. Take care."

"Send Zoe my love and tell her I'm here if she needs me."

"I'll be sure to pass on your message."

Sam left the house via the same way and sought out Bob who was still talking to the two ladies he'd been chatting to all the time she'd been inside with Gillian.

"Can I have a word, Sergeant Jones?"

Her partner appeared relieved to be dragged away. "Yes, boss."

They took six or seven paces away from the women.

Sam lowered her voice and said, "I've got the details of the next of kin. We should get over there ASAP. Have you found out anything significant?"

"Not really, no."

"Okay, get onto the station, ask them to flood the area with uniforms to obtain the statements. Tell them to do a house-to-house enquiry, see if anyone else either heard or saw anything here either last night or first thing."

"Will do."

They made their way back to the cars under the gaze of the local residents, still rubbernecking the crime scene. Sam made a mental note to have a word with Des about the delay in covering the body in the alley. In her opinion, that should never happen, and she couldn't help wondering what was going on in his head, causing a possible distraction. But that could wait, they had bad news to break to the victim's daughter.

Sam sighed and slipped behind the steering wheel of her new car. The insurance company had finally paid out after her old car had been destroyed by her late husband's selfish act. The decision had been a tough one, and Rhys, her boyfriend, had helped her finally decide on a Toyota Corolla. She wanted to be more conscious of the environment, so this time had chosen a hybrid car. Although she'd only had it a few weeks, she was used to it and found it a dream to drive. Even though Bob said the interior was smaller than that of her previous car and complained his head always touched the roof. But then, Bob was that sort, a moaning minnie as she liked to call him. She felt thankful that he was driving his own car for the trip ahead.

BOB PULLED up alongside her in the small car park across the road from the baker's. They met up again and crossed the busy road. The goodies on display in the shop window made Sam's stomach rumble; it wouldn't be right to buy anything, not after breaking the sad news to Zoe. Sam set her craving for sugary food aside and opened the door. Three customers formed a queue at the counter. Sam and Bob joined the end of it. Two assistants filled the customers' orders, so they didn't have to wait that long.

The taller of the two assistants smiled and walked towards them. "Hi, what can I get you this morning?"

Sam produced her warrant card and asked, "Are you Zoe?"

"Umm... yes, I am. Why are you here?" Her cheeks suddenly drained of all colour, and her gaze darted around the other customers and her colleague.

"Is it possible to speak to you in private? I appreciate how busy you are, but it's really important."

"Fiona, can you cope for a few minutes? I can ask Ray to drop what he's doing out the back to come and lend you a hand, if you like?"

"Go. I'm fine. The rush is almost over. Do what you have to do, Zoe."

"Thanks." Zoe pointed to the other end of the counter at a gap by the till. "Do you want to come through?"

Sam and Bob walked past the inquisitive queue of people and followed Zoe into an open area at the back.

"What's this all about?"

"Can we take a seat first?" Sam asked, noting there were a few plastic chairs dotted around the room.

Bob gathered three of them together and set them out.

Zoe nodded. She swallowed. Sam feared the young woman was already sensing the worst. Zoe sat heavily in the chair opposite Sam and Bob and placed a hand on her right cheek.

"I know what you're about to tell me isn't good. Is it Mum?"

Sam gave a brief nod. "You're right, it's not. I'm sorry to have to inform you that your mother was found dead this morning."

"What? No, this can't be true. Not Mum." Zoe buried her head in her hands and sobbed.

It was a while before the sobbing died down. Sam was prepared to wait, she always felt bad rushing things when someone's world had imploded.

Zoe eventually dropped her hands into her lap and sniffed. "I warned her only last night to be careful on the walk home from work. Was she attacked?"

"Things are a little sketchy right now, but it would appear that your mother made it home last night. However, her body was moved after she was killed and left in the alley."

Zoe shook her head in confusion. "Why? I don't under-stand what you're telling me."

"That's how we found your mother, in the alley. Further investigation led us through the back gate of her house. That's where we discovered the murder scene, inside the house, in the living room."

"Murder... what you said is only just sinking. Who would...?" Her voice trailed off, and she glared at a stain in the carpet to her right. "It has to be them... him... he's done this to her. He must have done it."

"Who are you talking about, Zoe?"

The young woman fiddled with the clip holding her hair in place. After a while, she said, "My father."

"Is there a reason you would think that? Has he threatened your mother in the past? In recent days or weeks?"

"No, but I wouldn't put it past him. Mum didn't tell me everything that went on between them. She always said that she could handle him, only last night we were discussing the time they spent together... she told me she handed out as much as she got from him."

"He abused her?" Sam asked.

Bob whipped out his notebook.

"Yes. Throughout their marriage. I hate him for the way he treated her."

"Were they divorced or separated?"

"Divorced, for the past eighteen months."

"Was there a reason you were discussing your mother's past marriage with her last night?"

Zoe paused to contemplate. "I can't remember now."

"Did your mother have a job?"

"Yes, she worked at the Texaco garage not far from her house. I warned her about the dangers of walking home alone at night."

"Was there a reason why your mother chose to ignore your concerns?"

"Apart from her being stubborn, no, she always assured me she would be safe and that no one was likely to attack an old girl like her... and now this... she's gone... murdered. Why isn't it sinking in? I feel so damn useless, numb all of a sudden. Can I see her?"

"It's the shock. Unfortunately, you won't be able to see her until a post-mortem has been performed. That should take place in the next day or so. I'll pass on your details to the pathologist, he'll be in touch advising you when you can see her. Is that all right?"

"It's going to have to be, isn't it? If that's the procedure. How? How was she killed?" She wiped the tears away with her sleeve and sniffed again.

"Her throat was cut, and it would appear she had been stabbed multiple times."

Zoe's hand covered her eyes again, and her shoulders jiggled. "How horrendous, to take my mother's life like that. Do you know if she put up a fight?"

"We don't, not yet. That sort of information will come out during the post-mortem. Don't worry, we'll get to the bottom of this."

"How can you say that? Are you going to go after him? My father?"

"He will be the first person we interview about the crime."

"Interview, is that it? You need to drag him into the station and lock him up, that'd teach him a bloody lesson. Oh, and be warned, he's a fucking liar. Has been all his life. He's not about to change now either, so you'd better be on your game when you question him. He's done this, there's no fucking doubt in my mind about that."

"Unfortunately, without any solid evidence to back up your claim, it's going to be difficult to prove."

"What? You don't believe me, is that what you're saying?"

"No, I'm not. Don't get me wrong, I will question him, but that might be as far as it goes if he has an alibi."

"An alibi? Jesus, he has contacts, any one of his friends might have gone over there and killed Mum, so what if he has a damn alibi?"

"If that's the case, the truth will come out in the end. That's a highly unusual scenario, one that only seems to come up in TV shows or films. It's our job to sift through the facts. At present, we have little to no factual evidence to go on. We've spoken to your mother's immediate neighbours. No one either heard or saw anything around the time of the... incident."

"You mean the murder, surely?" Zoe replied sharply. "Let's not forget that my mother's life was taken deliberately last night, it's not like she died of natural causes."

"I'm not. I apologise if it came across as that. I tend to guard my words when dealing with the next of kin, not everyone can take the facts as they are, not while the grief is setting in."

"And now you're saying that this hasn't affected me? Jesus, where do you get off coming here and speaking to me like this? I've offered you a possible suspect's name, you should be out there, chasing it up. Instead you're here, dithering, digging yourself a massive hole. And yes, I'm pissed off, wouldn't you be? If your mother's life had just been extinguished in the vilest possible way?"

"I would. I think we seemed to have got off on the wrong foot. I'm so sorry if I've upset you at all, that truly wasn't my intention."

"Then why won't you listen to me and arrest my father?" Zoe's stare intensified.

Sam fidgeted in her seat and let out the breath she'd sucked in moments earlier. "As I've already stated, we will visit your father next, but without any evidence placing him at the scene, we won't be able to proceed further."

"That's utter bollocks, and you know it. You have the power to arrest anyone if you believe them to be in the wrong."

"You're right, we do, however, if we want the case to stand up in court there are procedures in place that we need to stringently follow. If you want to take the risk of things backfiring on us, I'll willingly go over there and arrest him, if you think it will make you feel any better." Sam knew she was pushing the boundaries with Zoe, there was no way she would be willing to do such a thing, but if that's what Zoe wanted to hear at this time, then so be it.

Zoe gritted her teeth and shook her head. "You do what you need to do. Just be warned, he has a way with words. He tied me and my mother up with them many a time over the years."

"Don't worry, we're dab hands at dealing with different people right across the spectrum. Do you have his address?"

Zoe removed her phone from inside her uniform and glanced over her shoulder. "I hope the boss doesn't see me, we're not supposed to have our phones with us behind the counter." She scrolled through her contacts and brought up the number and address of her father. She angled the phone in Bob's direction so he could note it down.

"Thanks. Is there anything else you can tell us about your father?"

"He's a bastard. That's probably not the type of thing you want to hear, is it?"

Sam smiled. "I'd rather make up my own mind about what type of character he is. I meant, does he have any issues that might lead someone to want to disrupt his life in any way?"

Zoe frowned. "You've lost me. How is killing my mother going to disrupt his life? Surely, it's only going to enrich it, right? Which is why his name should be at the top of your suspect list."

"What I'm trying to ascertain is whether your father has done anything that could be perceived as dodgy, breaking the law, that might come back to haunt him." As soon as the words left her mouth, Sam knew that Zoe was going to blast her once more.

"I repeat, why should anything he's been in trouble for

come down heavily on my mother and not his bit on the side?" Zoe clicked her finger and thumb together. "That's it, if it's not him, then it could be her."

"Your father's new partner?"

"Yes. Helen Ridgway, that's her name. You can do all sorts of background checks on her, can't you?"

"We can, and we will, you have my assurance of that. Is there anything else you can tell us about either of them?"

"Plenty, but my language wouldn't be very ladylike. You'll get what I mean when you lay eyes on the despicable couple. Vile, they are, they bloody deserve each other. Mum did the right thing kicking that lowlife out of the house, eventually."

"Is there no way back for you two? Just because your parents had fallen out of love with each other, that doesn't mean that your relationship with your father should suffer."

"Nope. He made his feelings known when I stuck by Mum. I don't want to know him, he disgusts me. Turns my stomach every time I lay eyes on him."

"That's a shame. Maybe there will be hope of a reconciliation in the future for the pair of you."

"I'm not holding my breath, not while he's with her. She's pure evil, she is. Like I said before, they deserve each other. Are you going to go and see him now? He should be there, he usually does the evening shift in his cab. See, he was probably on duty when she was likely killed, another strike against his name in my book, that is."

"We'll be on our way soon. First, I need to ask you a few more questions about your mother."

"Such as?"

"Did she ever have any problems whilst working at the petrol station? I'm presuming she worked the evening shift there, is that correct?"

"It is. No, she would have told me. She always said the time went quickly, especially during the week. She loved it

29

there, the punters all had a laugh with her. She told me the banter was second to none. It was that place that kept her spirits up when she was with Dad."

"So they both worked the evening shift? What about caring for you?"

"No, Mum used to work days back when they were together, so there was always someone at home with me. It was the overlapping time in between when they were both at home that ended up destroying their marriage. It was like World War Three had started within our four walls, every single day of my life. I put the flags out the day they said they were getting a divorce, even though it took them another ten years to get around to finalising the paperwork."

"Ten years... ouch. And during that time, was your father seeing this Helen, or were there other women involved before she came along?"

"One or two, I reckon, over the years. A man like that can never remain faithful."

"Did your mother mention feeling anxious at all in the last week or so, as if someone was following her?"

"No, never. Mum was a very confident woman. She carried pepper spray in her handbag. I was always on at her about her safety at night. She assured me she had it covered..." Zoe's head dropped. "I can't believe I will never see her again. Life sucks when you least expect it. Why? Why take her life? She had nothing, except the house. Nothing of value there, inside."

"Ah, that was going to be my next question. When we briefly searched the house, we found a couple of shoeboxes in the bottom of her wardrobe that had been disturbed. Do you have any idea what might be missing?"

Zoe glanced up, and a frown pinched her brow. "How the heck should I know? I haven't seen the contents of those boxes in years. It was all Mum's personal paperwork. Are you suggesting that she disturbed a burglar and they killed her?"

Sam shrugged. "We don't know, it's a distinct possibility. What we're having trouble understanding is why the killer would have chosen to move your mother's body. As far as we could tell, and we only carried out a brief assessment of the property, is that the two boxes were the only items that appeared to have been touched."

Zoe hitched up her shoulders. "I can't help you. My mother kept all her personal paperwork in those boxes, and they were always treated that way, personal and private, so there's no way of me knowing if there will be anything missing."

"Don't worry. We'll set that aside for now. Are you going to be all right? Do you have other family members you can be with at this time?"

"No, there was just me and Mum. We lost my grandparents when I was around ten, they had a road accident and were both in a coma for a few months until their machines were turned off. Broke Mum in two, losing them around the same time in such horrific circumstances. Still, I think it gave her the strength to finally call it a day with Dad, so that's one good thing that came out of the ordeal we all had to endure."

"Glad there was a positive to cling to. We're going to head over to your father's now. Thanks for sharing all the background information with us. I'll give you one of my cards. If you should think of anything else, please get in touch."

Sam handed Zoe a business card and left her seat. Bob flicked his notebook shut, popped it in his pocket and joined her at the doorway into the shop. They left Zoe, sitting there, bewildered. She didn't acknowledge them further before they left.

The shop was empty.

The other assistant came forward to speak with them. "Is

31

everything all right? The boss was angry that Zoe had left me alone in the shop, but he backed off when I told him you were here to see her and it looked serious."

"We had to share some grave news about a family member. My advice would be to give her five minutes' alone time and then check in on her. Please pass on my apologies to your boss. Unfortunately, sharing news of this nature can't be delayed."

"Oh dear. Family member? It's no one too close, is it?"

Sam smiled. "Sorry, it's not for me to divulge that news. I'm sure Zoe will tell you if she wants you to know."

The colour flushed in the young woman's cheeks. "Sorry if you think I'm being nosey, I'm concerned, that's all."

"I know. If you're close, I'm sure Zoe will tell you when the time is right."

"Oh, we are. I'll be here for her, don't worry."

Sam smiled and walked towards the front door. It opened, and another glut of customers filled the small shop area.

"Sorry, if you'll let us squeeze through. Thanks."

Outside, Bob brushed himself down and said, "Blimey, are people really that eager to get their daily bread and cake supply?"

"If it's that busy, I bet they run out quickly."

During a lull in the traffic, they trotted across the road to the cars.

"It didn't look that good to me," Bob grumbled.

Sam raised an eyebrow. "Really? If I went back and ordered a dozen filled rolls and doughnuts, are you telling me you'd turn down your share?"

"Did I say that?" He rubbed his stomach.

"You're incorrigible. I'll follow you as you've got the address."

"Makes perfect sense to me."

CHAPTER 2

*T*he house was on a council estate, tucked towards the back of a small cul-de-sac. It was neatly presented with a small garden at the front on either side of what appeared to be a newly laid brick path. The tell-tale sign that Brian Callard was at home was the black taxi parked half on the pavement outside the house.

"Curtains are closed upstairs. He ain't gonna be happy to see us if we disturb his sleep," Bob said.

"Oh well, we'll soon see if that's the case. Ring the bell, Sergeant, make yourself useful."

"Ha, bloody cheek. I'm useful every minute of the day, always have been."

Sam turned her head to the side and mumbled, "If you say so."

Bob rang the bell and immediately looked up at the window. "Oops, he was asleep, he ain't any more."

"Great. That's got to be a top tip in the 'How to win friends and influence people handbook', right? Not to wake someone up when they've got in late the previous night."

The door was wrenched open before Bob had a chance to reply.

Sam held up her warrant card and shoved it in the man's face which was beet red with anger. "DI Sam Cobbs. It is Mr Callard, isn't it?"

"Yeah, that's right. Make it snappy, I was in bed, and no, I'm not a lazy bastard, I didn't get in until three this morning. I had a late airport run to Newcastle, can't refuse a big job like that these days, even if it came through around eleven o'clock."

Alarm bells rang in Sam's head. *I need Des to come up with a time of death ASAP.* "All right if we come in for a quick chat? We won't keep you long, I promise."

He pulled the door closed behind him and shook his head. "You're not coming in, not until you tell me why you're here."

"It's a personal matter. It would be better if we spoke in private, unless you want your neighbours earwigging our conversation."

"Do I fuck. You'd better come in. I need to sling some clothes on. Take a first right, into the lounge, I'll be with you shortly." He took flight up the stairs in his vest and boxer shorts.

Sam pushed open the door and was surprised to find the lounge tidy but then she remembered there was supposed to be a woman living in the house as well. She circled the room, picking up the odd photo frame of Callard with a woman who seemed to have dyed hair. Either that or she was possibly an alien, with her strands of purple locks interspersed with jade green. They seemed happy enough, in their own way.

Callard thundered back down the stairs, and he appeared in the doorway, wearing a thick pullover and faded jeans.

"Take a seat. Anywhere but the cracked leather armchair. I've got it nice and comfortable now, took years, believe me."

"Thanks. The sofa will do fine. Mr Callard, we've just come from visiting your daughter, she gave us your address."

His eyes narrowed, and he scratched his neck. Sam wondered if it was a nervous reaction.

"Oh, why would she do that?" He gave a slight cough to clear his throat.

Sam maintained eye contact with him for a few moments and then said, "We're heading up a murder inquiry."

He sat on the edge of his seat, and his head craned forward. "A what? Who?"

Again, Sam latched on to his gaze as she revealed the truth. "Your ex-wife."

He launched himself out of the chair and paced the floor in front of Sam and Bob.

"Sit down, Mr Callard," she advised. She sensed her partner getting anxious beside her.

"And you've come here? Why? Why would Zoe point you in my direction?"

"Sit down, sir, and we'll discuss this issue rationally."

"Issue? What, of my ex being murdered? Sorry, but that *issue* as you call it, has just knocked me bloody sideways. Tell me how I'm supposed to act. It's obvious my daughter has thrown my sodding name into the hat the first chance that came her way. Jesus."

"The inspector asked you to take a seat, and now I'm telling you to," Bob said sternly.

Sam nudged his knee to let him know that she had everything under control, at least she thought she had.

Relenting, Callard returned to his chair and apologised. "This is such a shock. I'm not going to ask the obvious question, like who did it, because you wouldn't be sitting here if you knew that, would you? And no, it wasn't me, I swear it wasn't. When did it happen?"

"We're still awaiting the actual time of death, but it was either last night or in the early hours of this morning."

He pointed, and his finger bounced up and down. "If that's the case, then I have my alibi all sewn up. I've already told you I was on an airport run between eleven and three this morning. That should be good enough for you."

"We'll need to drop by your firm and corroborate the facts with your boss."

"You do that. Is that it? Can I get back to bed now?"

Sam raised an eyebrow. "Don't you care? That your daughter has lost her mother, that your ex-wife has lost her life?"

Callard fell back in his chair and crossed his arms in defiance. "Should I? I owe that woman nothing. The years I spent in that suffocating marriage. I couldn't wait to leave her in the end. She got the house out of me. I left it all behind and started afresh."

"With someone else," Sam added quickly.

"What if I did? Helen and I were always meant to be together. Tammy was an obstacle in the way."

Sam inclined her head. "An obstacle in the way? As in you couldn't wait to get rid of Tammy? Her death would give you free rein to live your life with Helen, am I right?"

He bounced upright and pointed at Sam. "Now you listen to me, that's not what I said... well, maybe I did, but you've gone and twisted my words. I did not *kill* Tammy."

"And you're remorseful that she's passed, is that what you're going to say next?"

"Fuck you! I have no regrets leaving that woman, never have had. Don't come here expecting me to show her sympathy when she made my life a living hell, got that?"

"All right, calm down, mate," Bob interjected.

"I'm not your frigging mate, never will be. I've heard what you lot are capable of, fitting innocent folks up... well, think again, you won't get away with it this time. My alibi is set in stone, so get around that one if you can."

Sam faced Bob and placed her finger against her cheek. "He's pretty convincing, isn't he? Does he think we're stupid? That our IQ is below seventy or what?"

Bob shrugged. "I know something, he needs to watch his mouth or he's going to talk himself into trouble."

"That's a wise piece of advice, Sergeant."

"Get knotted. I can tell what's going on here, and it ain't going to wash with me." Callard seethed, "Get out of my house. Now."

"If you eject us, it's a possible sign that you know more than you're letting on, Mr Callard," Sam warned.

"How do you make that one out? I repeat, I have a solid alibi, not that you're prepared to bloody listen to me. Even I can't be in two places at once."

"No, maybe not, but that doesn't mean that you're not behind the murder."

He shot out of his chair again and took two paces towards Sam.

Bob jumped out of his seat and held a hand against Callard's chest, preventing him from getting any closer. "Sit down and calm down."

"This is my house. I'll do what I want in it. You're both sitting here accusing me of doing something that, first, I'm not capable of doing, and second, I wasn't even in Workington at the time she was bloody murdered, and third, if I'm hearing right, you're suggesting that I what? Paid for her to be bumped off? Why? Why would I do that when I left everything behind for her? Why?" He peered around Bob's stocky frame and looked Sam in the eye.

"It's a line of questioning we need to explore. There was

obviously a lot of animosity between you and Tammy, it's only natural for us to believe you might have something to do with her death, either directly or indirectly."

He fell into his comfy chair again, and Bob retook his seat beside Sam.

"What's that supposed to bloody mean? Are you suggesting I've conjured up thousands of pounds to pay for someone to kill her? What the actual fuck are you talking about?"

"What about Helen, where was she last night?"

He shrugged and exhaled an exasperated breath. "How the fuck should I know? We're not tied at the hip. She does her thing and I do mine. It's the way we set out to be from the beginning. I got my freedom from Tammy and have no intention of allowing anyone else to tie me down, if you get my drift?"

"I do. Is she around?" Sam asked.

"She's still asleep upstairs."

"Would you mind waking her up? If we can get this sorted today, it will make our investigation run a lot smoother."

"On your head be it, she's a nightmare in the mornings before she's downed a couple of mugs of coffee."

"I know that feeling. I'm willing to take the risk. Sergeant, can you put the kettle on?"

Bob stared at Sam in disgust after Callard left the room.

"You can't be serious? You want me to make the drinks?"

Sam smiled. "Thanks, you read my mind."

He got to his feet and mumbled something incoherent as he strolled towards the door. Sam took the time to walk a circuit of the room, picking up a picture frame here and there, seeing if she could see into the couple's souls through their photos. Raised voices sounded overhead, and she prepared herself for another barrage of anger once Helen eventually entered the room. Drawers and doors slammed, and within a few minutes, Callard returned to the room.

"She ain't happy and, in the circumstances, who could blame her? Where's your mate?"

"He's making a drink for all of us."

"Jesus, you've got a nerve, talk about taking the piss. Did I offer you a drink?"

Sam grinned, trying to cut through his anger. "No, which is why he's taken it upon himself to make one."

"He won't find anything, not in that kitchen."

"I'd suggest you give him a hand then." Sam beamed, showing off her pearly-white teeth.

Callard left the room, mimicking the way Bob had departed. Moments later, the woman with purple hair and vivid green highlights entered the room.

"Hi, I'm Detective Inspector Sam Cobbs. My partner and Mr Callard are in the kitchen."

"Why? What are they doing out there, except possibly making a mess?"

"More than likely. Men don't tend to be as domesticated as women, do they?"

"You can say that again. Why are you sitting in my house?"

Before Sam could explain, the door opened again, and Bob and Callard entered, carrying four mugs between them. Bob handed Sam a mug and sat beside her.

"Here you are, love, just how you like it, strong and sweet." Callard pecked Helen on the cheek and invited her to sit in his chair.

"You never give up your chair. What's going on around here? I demand to know!" Helen's countenance reflected her angry tone.

"Now, I need you to keep calm, love," Callard said, his

39

voice trembling, which surprised Sam, given the way Callard had been full of bravado in Helen's absence.

"Just tell me, Brian."

"I've got... some bad news," Callard stuttered.

"Don't hang around, get on with it, man," Helen said. She blew on her coffee and took a sip, her gaze flitting between Callard, Sam and Bob.

"It's Tammy..."

"What about that bitch, what has she done now?"

Callard winced at the harshness behind his girlfriend's words. "She's dead. Murdered, she was."

"Oh, right. And?"

"And, the police are here as part of their investigation."

"You mean they're here to point the finger at you," Helen corrected.

"That's not likely to happen, I have an alibi for when the murder was committed." His head bowed.

Helen glanced at Sam and then back at Callard. "You're not making any sense, what are you saying?"

He inhaled a deep breath and let it out slowly then said, "They're going to check on my alibi, but in the meantime... they umm... wanted to have a quick word with you."

"About her murder? What the fuck would I know about it?" The penny seemed to drop then, and Helen sneered at Sam. "You think I'm behind her death, don't you? What the fuck? How dare you come here and accuse me of doing such a thing? When? When did she die?"

"We've yet to have that confirmed, it should become clearer after the post-mortem."

"Which will happen when?"

"Hopefully later today."

"And you've got the audacity to show up here, accusing me of killing that bitch. And yes, I'm not denying I hated her, but I'm not a damn murderer. I wouldn't know where to bloody begin for a start. You can't show up here, throwing these types of accusations around, can you? Not at decent folks like us, surely?"

"It would be wrong of us not to ask the question."

"Sorry, I don't agree. I think it's wrong of you to blatantly turn up at my house and badger us like this. Go and do your detective work elsewhere because there is nothing for you here." She stood and walked across the room to the door. "I'm going back to bed, don't disturb me again."

"We either complete the interview here or we take this down the station, Helen, the choice is yours," Sam said. "An informal interview is always preferable in my opinion."

"Are you threatening me?" Helen ground her teeth.

Sam's mouth turned down at the sides, and she shook her head. "No, merely stating facts."

"You can't force your way into this house and expect me to be dancing around with joy. I'm going to report you to your senior officer."

"Which you're entitled to do, except, let me correct you on a minor detail, we didn't force our way in here, Mr Callard invited us in."

Helen glared at Callard. "You moron. You should've refused to let them in. There's no getting rid of the filth once they set foot inside your house."

"That's grossly unfair, Helen," Sam replied, offended by the woman's choice of words.

"Tough. It's the truth. I've met your type many a time over the years."

Sam tilted her head and frowned. "You have? Do you want to tell me under what circumstances?"

Helen shuffled nervously by the door but remained silent.

Callard approached her and flung an arm around her shoulders. "Give her a chance, love. She's only doing her job."

Which knocked Sam back. She hadn't expected to see the sudden change of heart in him.

Helen sighed and relented. She returned to her seat with Callard's arm still draped around her shoulders. "What do you want from us? From me?"

Sam combatted the woman's harsh tone with a smile. "All we're after is information."

"About?" Helen asked, her temples being distorted by a severe frown.

"About Tammy's murder."

"There you go again… it's as if you think we're behind it, *we're not*. Brian was on a late trip to the airport, and I waited up, watching TV until I fell asleep in the chair. Where did it happen? At work?"

"No. Her death occurred while she was at home, but the killer chose to move her body into the alley, possibly to deflect the crime. We have no way of knowing that until we track the killer down and question them."

"Do you always assume the ex has killed the victim? Is that customary for the police?"

"Sometimes."

"Crap, and this is one of those times?"

"Zoe gave them our address," Callard answered.

"What? Your own daughter put your name forward for this godawful crime? Why aren't you livid?"

"Inside I am, but what's the point in getting riled up about it? We both know she hates my guts, she's proved that over the last year or so."

"Care to enlighten us as to what you mean by that?" Sam asked, quickly jumping in before yet another argument erupted between the couple.

"We've had hateful messages via email and text, all deleted now because why keep something so full of anger and hatred? It was only a matter of time before she overstepped the mark, and I guess this is it. How appalling for her to put her own father in the frame for murder. That girl has got a bloody screw loose, she's the one who needs locking up... in an asylum."

"Don't, Helen. You know how much I love her, she's my daughter. Whether she's been a pain in the arse or not. Looking at this from her point of view, she's bound to put my name forward."

"She might do, but I'll not get dragged into it, you hear me, Brian? I didn't sign up for this shit. My days of dealing with the cops are over."

Brian rolled his eyes to the ceiling, but it was Sam who spoke next.

"You've been in trouble with the police before, I take it?"

Helen took a sip from her mug. A defeated expression crossed her features. "I was on the game. You'll do the necessary digging when you get back to the station, so I might as well tell you now. I used to be the local bike."

"For fuck's sake, what have I told you about saying that?" Brian snapped.

"All right, let's not start flinging names at each other or ripping one another to shreds," Sam insisted. "When was this, Helen?"

"My last trick was a couple of years ago... it was him."

Callard placed his hands over his face. "Thanks, you could have left that bit out."

"Why do you always have to be ashamed about finding needs elsewhere if you weren't getting the proper attention from her at home?"

"It's embarrassing... going with a prostitute."

"We have needs, too. My need was to keep this roof over my head. I had to do whatever I could for that to happen. I'm not ashamed to tell people the depths I've had to resort to in order to come good again."

"I suppose," Callard admitted. He gripped her free hand and kissed the back of it in a loving gesture.

"I have to ask, when you were living with Tammy, whether you had any problems... let me clarify, any aggro with anyone who would likely want to kill your ex-wife?" Sam asked, eager to get back on track with the investigation.

He took a moment to contemplate and then shook his head. "Not that I can think of."

"What about that job of hers?" Helen suggested. "She always tended to volunteer to do the night shift after Brian left, it depends on what type of customer she got down there at the petrol station."

"We've yet to visit her place of work. No doubt there will be CCTV footage we can look over, see if anything shows up there. I just wondered if there had been anything in her personal life that we could delve into."

"Not that I can think of," Callard replied. "Your best bet is going to see her boss. We've got nothing to hide and definitely had nothing to do with her murder."

Sam believed him. "We'll check it out. How long were you married?"

Brian puffed out his cheeks and tipped his head back. "Zoe is twenty-five, we were married a couple of years before she came along."

"Was Tammy involved with anyone else before you two started going out together?"

"One or two. Nothing major, the odd night out here and there. Why?"

"We often get revenge attacks, you know, previous partners entering a person's life when they find them back on the market again." Sam shrugged. "It was just a thought."

"I don't think so. I've not heard about either of the blokes after we got wed. If Tammy had seen them around town when we were together, she didn't tell me. Maybe

Zoe can fill in the blanks of what happened after we split up."

"I'll make a note to ask her. What about friends, had she fallen out with anyone in recent years?"

"Not that I can remember. Again, maybe you should be directing that sort of question at Zoe instead of me."

"Yes, that's right. He can't answer your questions, he stopped being interested in what she either said or did a few years before their marriage ended," Helen added sarcastically.

Sam took the hint and decided to leave the interview there, rather than cause the couple any more upset. "Thanks for your assistance. I'm going to give you one of my cards in case you happen to think of anything that might help with our investigation."

"We won't," Helen replied without hesitation.

Sam and Bob found their own way to the door, leaving behind the couple who were discussing the issue with raised voices. Sam closed the front door and they walked back to the cars in silence.

"She comes across as a hard woman," Bob muttered.

"You read my mind. Something is not quite right there. We need to get back to the station and start digging."

"You think she's behind the murder?"

Sam shrugged. "I'm not sure. There was obviously no love lost between her and Tammy, how deep that went is anyone's guess."

"Hmm... I suppose it's better to have a suspect on our radar this early on than nothing at all."

"I'll meet you back at the station."

Sam jumped in her car and started the engine. During the journey, she reflected on what they had learnt so far about the victim and her family. Which didn't really amount to much as yet. The issue that troubled her most was the fact the victim's body had been moved and left in the alley. Why? It was unusual for a killer to move a body from the original crime scene. She had known the odd occasion over the years, but the victim's body was found a fair distance from the original murder scene. Why?

The real work began once they were back at the station. Sam still remained thoughtful as she ran through what had occurred that morning with the rest of the team.

"Is something wrong?" Bob asked once she'd set everyone a task.

"Something is puzzling me."

"Are you going to tell me what that is or are you expecting me to guess? How many guesses do I get?"

She tutted. "Maybe it's just me, but I don't recall seeing her mobile either at the scene with her body or in the house."

Bob shrugged. "Maybe she didn't have one, it's not obligatory, you know."

Sam pulled a face at him. "Really? How many people do you know who don't have a mobile these days?"

Bob raised a finger as he thought. "Well, it took my mum years of me nagging her to finally break down and get one. Even now she only uses it for emergencies. Hates using it, tells me it's the worst invention of all time."

"I have to agree sometimes. It bugs me the way people have become so reliant on them these days."

"Whatever. I have peace of mind knowing that Abigail and Milly both carry theirs everywhere with them."

Sam sighed. "But we're talking about a different generation. The victim was older, what? In her fifties? I know that's not regarded as old these days, but people of that age don't tend to be over-reliant on their phones compared to someone of our age."

"Says you. We're talking ten to fifteen years' difference, in case you need reminding. That's hardly anything."

"Silly me. All right, I'm guilty of going off on a tangent there for a moment. The crux of the matter is, I don't recall seeing one. I'm going to ring Des, see if any of the forensic team have picked it up." Sam walked into her office and rang Des from her landline. "Hi, just a quick query, I appreciate how busy you are."

"Who is this?" Des asked. He sounded distracted.

"Sorry, I should have said. It's me, Sam."

"Ah, okay. What do you want, Sam? I'm up to my eyes in it here."

"I'll be quick, I promise. I was wondering if you've discovered the victim's mobile."

There was a brief pause before he answered, "Can't say I have. I'm searching through the evidence bags now and can confirm there's nothing here. Why?"

"It's just something that's niggling me, that's all. Okay, I'll let the desk sergeant know and get his lads to do a sweep of the alley."

"If it means that much to you then so be it. Are we done here?"

"We are. Thanks for sparing me a second of your valuable time."

"It was more than a second, and you're welcome."

The line went dead, and Sam hung up. She immediately made another call to the front desk where she requested a search of the area once SOCO were out of the way. The desk sergeant told her not to worry, her request would be implemented ASAP.

Sam then tackled her daily mountain of paperwork but set the timer on her phone for thirty minutes. After that, she was determined to rejoin her team, to see if they had any results for her. She glanced around her desk and realised she didn't have a coffee to hand. She remedied that, then got on with her chores.

Bob was talking with Claire when she came out of her office.

"Something wrong?" Sam asked.

"Quite the opposite. Claire's managed to dig up quite a rap sheet for Helen," Bob replied, smiling.

Claire handed Sam a piece of paper, and she ran her gaze over it, after which she let out a whistle. "Bloody hell, even if her attitude hadn't caused my suspicion gene to be on full alert, this definitely does. Ten arrests over twelve years, mostly for prostitution and a couple of later arrests that are drug related. Interesting stuff."

"But she's kept her nose clean for the past couple of years," Claire was quick to add.

"Yeah, at least that's one thing in her favour," Sam agreed.

"But she'd have people in the know, the underground who'd be willing to bump someone off... at a price," Bob rested his backside on the desk behind him and chipped in.

"Yep, I'm with you on that one. Can we try and track down any known associates of hers?" Sam asked.

"Leave it with me, boss. I'll see what I can come up with." Claire smiled and tapped away at the keys on her computer.

"Any luck with finding cameras in the area?" Sam asked Bob.

"Liam and Oliver are dealing with that. Boys, anything yet?" Bob shouted across the room at their two younger colleagues.

"We've managed to track down who we suspect to be the victim after she left the petrol station from the cameras on the main road. She stopped to speak with a couple of youngsters who appeared to be the worse for wear then carried on walking. She turned off the road there. We're searching for any other available cameras in the area to see if we can pick her up again."

"Okay, stick with it. If all else fails, we've got a heads-up on the route she took home. It might be worth knocking on a few doors in the area, see if they have any cameras. If we get nothing from that, then I'll consider holding a dreaded press conference. I always prefer to hold off on them for as long as possible, but if the need arises, I'll do it for the cause."

"That's magnanimous of you," Bob mumbled.

Sam dug him in the ribs. "I think we should grab an early lunch and then nip over to the garage, see what her boss has to say."

"Sounds like a plan. What do you want, and I'll nip out to the baker's?"

"Wow, are you buying?"

"Did I say that? Go on then, if I must."

"I fancy an egg mayo on brown, a roll will do, thanks."

Bob collected the orders from the rest of the team and left. Sam took the opportunity to bring the whiteboard up to date. She jotted down the details of what she'd learned about the victim thus far and also noted down the names of Brian Callard and Helen Ridgway as possible suspects. Although her doubts were wavering slightly on those two, she knew it would be remiss of her not to keep them in the frame, for now at least.

AFTER DEVOURING THEIR LUNCH, Sam and Bob hit the road again. This time they chose to go in Sam's car to the victim's workplace. The petrol station was fairly busy, every pump occupied when they pulled up. They parked alongside a black BMW and entered the bustling shop. The man behind the counter appeared to be harassed and was snapping at the customers if they wanted something other than paying for the fuel they'd had.

They joined the queue, and Sam flashed her ID at the man

in his early to mid-thirties. "DI Sam Cobbs, and this is my partner, DS Bob Jones. Is the manager around?"

"You're looking at him. What do you want?"

"A chat in private. Is there another member of staff on duty who can take over from you?"

"Not for at least ten minutes. I won't be able to hang around, I need to get back to the hospital to visit my wife, she's in labour, has been all through the night. I'm only here because one member of staff called in sick first thing. I'm waiting for another one to get back to me as well, I can't get her on the phone, though, which is a bummer. Step aside, I need to keep the queue down."

"We'll wait over here until you're free."

"You do that. Just fuel, was it?" he asked the next customer.

"He's a bunch of laughs," Bob whispered in her ear as they tucked into the gap at the side of the chiller cabinets, out of the way of the queue.

"Stressed out, I should imagine. I hope he can spare us enough time to discuss the investigation, I have a feeling our interview is going to take place at warp factor five if he has a baby on the way."

"Maybe we should leave it for now."

"I'd rather not. Any information he can give us is a bonus at this stage."

Not long after, a young man with spiky hair, wearing a Texaco T-shirt and jeans, entered the shop. He waved at the boss behind the counter and dipped through a door on the right. He emerged a few seconds later and took over from his boss who patted him on the shoulder before he left the secured till area.

"Right, now I'm free, what can I do for you?"

"Is there somewhere less public we can speak?"

"I've got an office, but it's that small only one person can fit in there at a time. What about outside?"

"Would you object to sitting in the car with us?" Sam asked.

"Why should I? Sounds good to me, it's just started raining. I must repeat, I can't spare you long, I need to get on my way soon. Promised my wife I would be there at one-thirty, as soon as Russ got here."

"We'll try not to delay you too long."

They left the shop, and Sam pressed her key fob to open the doors of her car.

"Sorry, I didn't get your name?"

Their visitor settled into the back seat, and Sam twisted in hers to speak with him.

"It's Blake... Blake Donald."

"All right if I call you Blake?"

"Sure. What's this about?"

"We're leading a murder inquiry and wondered if you could help us out with some information about the victim."

He frowned and inclined his head. "Victim, do I know him or her?"

Sam inhaled a large breath. "You do, we believe she's a member of your staff."

"What? Who?"

Sam watched carefully, gauging his reaction. "Tammy Callard."

His hand swept through his longish blond hair. "What the...? There must be some mistake. Wait, I've tried to call her this morning... no wonder I couldn't get an answer. How did she die? When?"

"Either late last night or in the early hours of this morning. Can you tell us at what time she finished her shift last night?"

"Midnight, or thereabouts. Christ, don't tell me she was attacked on the way home from work?"

"No, we believe she made it home and was killed there."

He glanced at his watch and asked, "How can I help?"

"You can tell us if she was alone on shift last night or if another member of staff was with her."

"Alone. There's not enough staff on the books for two of them to work alongside each other. We're having trouble recruiting people these days, just like everyone else supplying any form of customer service."

"I understand. Would you have any camera footage of the forecourts?"

"Yes, and inside the shop. Listen, I'd love to help out but I sense what you're asking is going to take time to sort out and I've already told you that time is against me."

"I know, I'm really sorry to put you in this position, but the delay might allow a killer to go free."

"God, now you're going to make me feel bad. Okay, we need to go back to the shop. I'll whiz through the discs for you. You think someone caused aggro in the shop and then followed her home?"

"It's a possibility. Any help you can give us would be appreciated."

"We'd better shake a leg then. Sorry, I should have said how upset I am that Tammy has died. I'm shocked that someone would think badly enough of her to want her dead. I hope it wasn't one of our customers who did this. She was doing me a favour last night, locking up. The takings were all there when I got in this morning, so it's not like we had a robbery and she had to hand over the money to save her life. It doesn't add up to me."

"Me neither. Maybe it was nothing to do with the petrol station, after all. If we can see the footage anyway, just to make sure?"

"Of course."

Blake got out of the back, and Sam opened her door.

She rested a hand on Bob's forearm and said, "You might as well stay here, there will probably only be room for Blake and me in his tiny room."

Bob raised an eyebrow. "Cosy. Okay."

"Idiot. I won't be long, because he keeps reminding me he has a baby on the way."

"Yeah, don't let the sprog drop before he gets there, his life won't be worth living if that happens. I should know, I missed Molly's birth by minutes, and Abigail never lets me forget the fact."

"Oh dear. I never knew that." Sam trotted to catch up with Blake. "Is this your first baby?"

"Yes. We've been trying for several years, was about to start IVF when Kelly fell pregnant. It's been a nightmare pregnancy for her, morning sickness, low iron levels throughout, so she's had to take things easy. That's why I'm eager to be with her."

"I won't detain you for long, I promise."

They walked through the now quiet shop and into a small office that didn't even have room for a desk.

"Crap, how do you manage to do your paperwork in here?"

"I don't. I always take it home with me."

"Ouch, I bet that goes down well with Kelly."

"Needs must as they say. Right, what do we have here?" He fiddled with the machine, swapped over the discs and ran through the footage. "Nothing out of order here, not unless you've spotted anything?"

"I haven't. Tammy seemed at home with the customers, jovial and very attentive to their needs."

"She was a lovely lady. I've never had any bother with her. She always dropped what she was doing to lend me a hand.

Unlike the others, she was truly dedicated to her job. Some people might not think this is a good job, working at a petrol station, but I always treat my staff well, unlike some others in the area."

"I have no doubt about it. Can you switch to the cameras covering the forecourt now? I've seen all I need to see here."

"Sure. Give me a sec."

He worked swiftly and set the new disc up. Again, there was nothing really to see. Sam noted the time on the clock. When Tammy locked up the shop and began the walk home it was twelve-fifteen.

"I've seen enough. I'd like to thank you for your time. One last question, has Tammy ever had any cause to complain about a customer coming on to her in recent months?"

"No, not that she ever confided in me."

"Thanks. I'm going to leave you my card. When life settles down a bit, in the next few days, can you ask the rest of your staff for me, give me a ring if anything comes to light?"

"I'll do it throughout the day. I can call the staff from the hospital, until the baby makes an appearance, and get back to you. I should imagine you'll be wanting the information as soon as possible, won't you?"

"It would be preferable. I didn't want you to feel I was putting you under unnecessary stress, though."

"It's fine. I'd like to do what I can to help your investigation, if you'll allow me to. I feel bad rushing you like this but I need to get on the road. You know when you get that feeling in your gut that something is about to happen?"

"All too well. Thanks again for all your help, and I hope the baby enters the world soon, for both your sakes. I should imagine your wife is fed up with dealing with all that pain by now."

"Put it this way, I'd hate to be in her shoes at this time. I think if it were down to men going through the pregnancies in this world there would be fewer babies born."

Sam laughed and shook his hand. "I think you might be right. Take care and good luck. Pass on my best wishes to your wife."

"Thanks, I will."

AT THE END OF A LONG, fruitless day, Sam drove home, her thoughts still very much with the victim and the mysterious way her body had been moved to outside the property. She suspected a long walk with Sonny would help put things right. Her face lit up when she saw Rhys's car parked outside her cottage. Doreen was in her usual position at this time of the day, standing at her lounge window, awaiting her arrival, and Sonny joined her, his paws on the windowsill, jumping up and down. *Always nice to have a welcoming committee to greet me.* She waved at Doreen and got out of the car.

"Hello, Sam, have you had a good day?" Doreen asked.

Sonny was squealing with delight and running around in circles, weaving in and out of Sam's legs to the point where she almost lost her balance. "Calm down, Munchkin. A so-so day, Doreen, I won't bore you with the details, not because I want to keep them from you, but because I haven't quite figured them out myself, yet."

"Ah, I'm sure you'll do that eventually. Rhys has only been here five minutes. He let himself in."

"Thanks, I gave him a key. Right, I hope this one has behaved himself for you today?"

"He's been a gem, as usual. No bother in the slightest. You go, have a good evening, dear."

"Thanks, Doreen. I'll pop my head in first and then take this tyke for a walk."

Sonny bounced around again when he picked up on the W word.

They both laughed.

"I think he's a tad eager, don't you?" Doreen observed.

"As usual. Thanks for all you do for us, Doreen. I know I say it every day, but I truly mean it."

Doreen reached out and touched Sam's forearm. "I know you do. Enjoy yourself, lovely."

"You, too. See you tomorrow at the usual time?"

"Of course, I'd be upset if I didn't have this angel for company every day. I must admit, I used to miss him when your brother-in-law was off work and able to look after him."

"Really? You should have said. See, I don't like to burden you all the time with Sonny, it's nice to have a break now and again."

"Speak for yourself. He's my lifeline during the day, he keeps me sane, and Ginger absolutely adores him."

Sam hugged Doreen. "I'm always at the end of the phone. I've always got time for you, don't be afraid to reach out."

Doreen waved her hand. "Nonsense. I'm all right. Get away with you. Off you go, don't leave that nice young man of yours waiting any longer."

"I won't. Thanks, Doreen. Remember what I said, ring me if you need me, that's an order."

"I will, now that you've told me to. Goodnight, Sam."

"See you in the morning. Enjoy your evening."

Sam slotted her key in the front door, and Sonny ran in ahead of her.

"Hey, you. Calm down. Yes, it's lovely to see you, too," Rhys said, his voice in the distance.

Sam went through to the kitchen and found him close to the cooker, with a mug on the worktop beside him. He was bent down making a royal fuss over Sonny, which gladdened

Sam's heart to see, after what had happened with Benji and the way Rhys had kept away from her for a few weeks, after he'd lost his treasured pet and best friend. She approached him, and they shared a kiss. Sonny trotted over to his food bowl and tapped it with his paw.

"Looks like someone is eager for some food," Rhys said.

"I need to take him for a walk first." She smiled. "I don't suppose you want to join us, do you?"

She sensed his hesitation before he accepted. "I'd love to. Are you going now, or should we get changed first?"

"I'll just fling on some wellies and my dog-walking coat, that'll do me, but your suit might get splashed."

"Give me two minutes. Do you think he'll behave himself in that time?"

"Leave him to me, I'll give him a handful of biscuits to be getting on with for now."

Rhys pecked her on the nose and swept out of the room.

Sam saw to Sonny's needs and then panicked about what to do for dinner. Rhys's arrival had been somewhat of a surprise. She hadn't been expecting him to drop by this evening at all. Since they had got back together, at Chris's funeral of all places, they had both agreed to take things slowly. She had finally given him a key at the weekend, and since then he had been either too scared or possibly felt too uncomfortable to use it.

He reappeared as Sonny was polishing off his handful of biscuits. "I'm ready when you are," he announced. He had brought over a few outfits and left them in the wardrobe. This reunion was all about taking things slowly between them.

They set off, Sonny happily trotting along on the lead between them.

Rhys held her hand and smiled, even though it had started to rain. "Sod's law, eh?"

"Yep, it's as though it waits for us to get out of the door before pouring down. We'll go to the park, the trees will protect us, kind of."

They upped their pace and made it to the park within a few minutes. Sam let Sonny off the lead. He ran over to the trees and glanced up at the huge trunk of his favourite one, on the lookout for the squirrels to chase.

Rhys fell quiet as soon as they entered the park gates. Sam suspected he was reflecting on the good times he'd had here with Benji before they'd met.

She hooked an arm through his. "I'm here if you ever want to talk about it. I know it's still very raw, it is for me, too. Hopefully, in time we'll be able to get past the trauma of it all."

He sucked in and let out the long breath. "I doubt it, the impact on my life was immeasurable... on yours, too. Sorry, that sounded selfish."

"It didn't, and I knew what you meant. Our emotions are never going to dwindle. It sounds silly, but I loved Benji almost as much as you did. I know I didn't have the privilege of knowing him for long but I really got to know him and love him in that short time."

Rhys stared off in the distance and swallowed.

When he didn't speak, she asked, "Are you all right?"

He shook his head and said, "I don't think I'll ever be all right again." Then he detached himself from her grasp and walked away.

She noted he chose to set off in the opposite direction to the bridge where they had shared their first kiss. His decision to leave left her wondering if she had done the right thing getting back together with him. It felt like he was still blaming her for something that had been totally out of her control. It hadn't been her who had lit the lighter in the car, it had been Chris. She sighed and decided to leave Rhys to sort through his own problems while she plucked a tennis ball from her pocket and played fetch with Sonny for a while. With Sonny exhausted, she headed home again and caught up with Rhys at the top of the next road.

She slid an arm through his, startling him. "Sorry, I didn't mean to sneak up on you like that, I thought you might have heard me coming."

"I didn't, but it's fine. I owe you an apology."

"You owe me nothing, Rhys, don't ever think that."

"I'm not sure I'll ever be able to go near that park ever again, it brings back too many memories. I know it was the first place we met, but that has been overshadowed by the grief. Please forgive me."

"There's truly nothing to forgive. It was thoughtless of me to drag you down there, we should have just wandered around the block instead."

"No, you shouldn't be expected to change your routine just because I'm being silly."

"Far from it. Grief is real, whether it is for a human or an animal. Benji wasn't just your dog, he was your best friend who had seen you through the good times and the bad. Hey, I shouldn't need to be telling you this, you're the psychiatrist, after all." She pecked him on the cheek and was relieved the gesture put a smile on his face. "Come on, let's see what we can conjure up together for dinner."

"Or I could take a trip out to our favourite Chinese and pick up a takeaway, unless you fancy going out for a meal?"

"A takeaway sounds just the ticket after the day I've had. I just want to snuggle up with you and Sonny, instead of dressing up to go out to a restaurant, especially on a crappy night like tonight."

"True enough. A takeaway it is. What do you fancy? This one is on me."

"Surprise me, we usually end up sharing anyway."

59

He smiled and unlocked his car. She watched him go with an unmistakable ache in her heart, the overwhelming feeling of desertion she had whenever he drove off.

Get a grip, girl. He's only going up the road. Is he? What if he decides never to come back? Is that how it's going to be from this day forward? Me wondering if he'll walk out on me again?

She pushed away the seeds of doubt running through her mind and opened the front door. Sonny ran ahead of her and into the kitchen. He stood by his towel by the back door, waiting to be dried.

"You're an angel. Maybe I should put one by the front door as well." She glanced over her shoulder at the small puddles Sonny had left in his wake.

By the time she had dried and fed him and run upstairs to slip into her onesie—it was never too early to put that on, in her opinion—Rhys had returned with their meal.

"I was the only one in there, which was a blessing, although the queue was starting to build when I left."

"I'll dish up while you dry off."

"If I ever dry off. I had to battle through one of those biblical-type downpours on the way back to the car. It only lasted a few seconds, but by golly, it nearly washed me away."

They settled down with a bottle of red and enjoyed their feast with Sonny lying at her feet, not begging but hopeful of any scraps they might leave.

CHAPTER 3

*S*am and the team picked up where they'd left off the day before in their search to learn the truth about Tammy Callard's murder.

"Any news on the hunt for her phone yet?" Sam asked, ever hopeful.

"Not yet. Want me to chase it up with the desk sergeant?" Bob asked.

"Might be a good idea. Let's face it, we've got very little else to go on right now."

Bob nodded and got on the phone right away. Sam listened in to the conversation and watched his eyes light up. He gave her the thumbs-up, and she punched the air.

It could only be a good thing to find it. It had been poking her like a stick, wondering why it wasn't found in the house or with her body in the alley. Wasn't it the norm to be glued to your mobile these days?

Bob ended the call. "It was found in one of the bins in the alley, so someone tried to do away with it."

"Hmm... is the desk sergeant sending it over to the lab?"

"He's on the ball with that one, it's already in hand."

"Good. I'll give them a ring to make them aware of how urgent it is that we get the results ASAP." Once she'd had a word in the right ear down at the lab and received the assurance that the analysis of the phone would be dealt with as an urgent matter, she returned to the incident room.

Bob was going through the info they had gathered on Brian Callard and Helen Ridgway. "What bugs me is that he gave up on his marriage to effectively set up home with a prostitute. It doesn't make sense to me."

Sam shrugged. "Ours is not to reason why or judge in these circumstances, each to their own. She's obviously got something that attracted him in the first place."

He opened his mouth to speak, and she could tell by the glint in his eye that whatever was about to tumble out of his mouth next would be crude.

"Don't even go there."

"You spoil all my fun."

"Hardly, I'm only with you around nine hours a day... umm... yeah, don't respond to that either."

Bob tipped back his head and laughed. "Okay, I won't. Has your opinion changed on the couple? Are they still up there, high on the list of suspects?"

"I haven't stumbled across anything else to point us in another direction as yet."

"Still early days, I suppose. What's next?"

"I wish I knew. We keep going over what we have to hand: the record of Helen Ridgway, the fact Brian's daughter, Zoe, detests the pair of them. Now we know Tammy left work just after midnight, any CCTV footage we can gather that shows her on the way home could prove very helpful. It's all we can do, for now. I know one thing for certain, we could do with a break to get the investigation going."

"I might have something for you, boss," Claire shouted.

Sam rushed over to the sergeant's desk. "Go on."

"I did the usual digging into the victim's finances and found this." Claire drew Sam's attention to the statement she had up on the screen.

"A transfer of funds to Secured Capital of twenty-five thousand pounds. She didn't look the type to have savings. Christ, how did that come out of my mouth? That's the kind of derogatory statement Bob would come out with, not me."

Claire chuckled. She tapped the desk with her pen. "The thing is, I've searched for the company and can't find it anywhere."

Sam frowned. "Have you gone down the usual routes, checked with Companies House?"

"All of it. Whether it has stopped trading now, I don't know."

"Get onto the bank, see what they're willing to divulge. When was the transaction made?"

"June last year. It's a sizeable amount. Some kind of investment fund perhaps? Maybe it's an offshore one, that's why it's not registered at CH."

"Possibly. I'll leave it with you. I know what, while you ring the bank, I'll give Zoe a call, see if she has any ideas on the subject." Sam walked back into her office and sat at her desk. She flipped open her notebook and dialled Zoe's number. "Hi, Zoe. Can you talk? Sorry, it's DI Sam Cobbs, we met yesterday."

"Oh, hi. Yes, I'm free to talk, I'm on a break. I haven't got long, though. Did you go and see him? My dad?"

"Yes, we paid him a visit after we left you."

"And? Was it him? I should imagine you get an instinct for this type of thing, don't you?"

"Usually. I have to tell you, I'm not sure what to think of him and his new girlfriend at this early stage."

"Bugger. Don't let them get into your head, they do that with me all the time. Plant a seed and let it fester there for a while. I'm sure they're behind it, I'm downright confident they are."

"Unless we find any evidence pointing us in their direction, that's going to be difficult to prove."

"All right. So, why are you calling me then?" Her tone was now cold and standoffish.

"We're going over your mother's finances, and something has caught our eye."

"I don't understand."

"On her statements, from last year, we noticed that she transferred twenty-five thousand pounds to a company called Secured Capital. Did she mention it to you at all?"

"What? No, who are they?"

"Ah, that's the thing, we're doing our very best to try to find out and drawing a blank at the moment."

"Are you telling me they've gone out of business?"

"That's unknown. The company wasn't registered with Companies House. We're making a call to the bank now, see if they can tell us more about the transaction. Some banks make you jump through hoops when you try to transfer funds, let's hope that's the case here."

"But twenty-five grand... that would have come to me, been my inheritance. I can't believe this. I didn't know she had that amount sitting in her account at one time."

"Ah, that's why I was calling. To see if you knew where the money had come from or if your mother had mentioned that she was going to invest any money she may have had."

"Invest? I don't know, I suppose it's likely. Gosh she never breathed a bloody word of it. As to where it came from... maybe after my grandparents died, perhaps she left Mum the money in her Will. If she did, Mum kept it quiet. Perhaps she thought if she said anything, Dad would get to hear about it and want part of it in the divorce settlement. She already wrangled the house out of him."

"Possibly. We'll do some more digging, see if we can trace where the funds came from in the first place. Sorry to have disturbed you."

"It's fine. I'm glad you got in touch, it means you're treating Mum's case as important."

"Never fear about that. How are you doing?"

"I'm coping. I'm at work. I know that probably seems like I'm being heartless, but I was struggling being at home, despite the boss telling me to take a few days off."

"It doesn't at all. In these circumstances, you need to do what's right for you. There are no rules set in stone because every person deals with grief differently."

"I thought as much. My colleagues keep whispering behind my back. I'm sure they think I'm a monster for continuing to work."

"I'm sorry. They have no right to judge you."

"That's people of today for you, everyone has an opinion on someone else's life."

"I think you're right. Any problems, please let me know. I'm here to support you, okay?"

"Thank you, that means a lot to me. All I need is for you to find my mother's killer, and soon."

"We're on the case, don't ever doubt that. I'll catch up with you shortly. Would it be all right to call you if something else crops up? Similar to this?"

"Of course, I'd be upset if you didn't. I want to help in any way I can. She should never have passed away like this. It still makes me shudder. Do you think I'll be able to see her soon? I know that sounds macabre but I need to say a personal goodbye to the woman I loved most in this world."

"I'll call the pathologist now and get an answer for you."

"I hope to hear from you soon."

"You will." Sam ended the call and immediately rang Des.

He answered after the fourth ring. "Des, it's Sam Cobbs. Sorry to disturb you, I have a strange request."

"Hmm... which is?"

"The victim from yesterday, Tammy Callard, I've just spoken to her daughter, and she's asked when it would be possible to see her mother."

"Not a strange request at all, they usually call us. I completed the PM this morning, left her to be sewn up by a member of my team. That should have been completed by now. You can tell her she can come in a few hours, that'll give us time to prepare the body."

"Midday then? She's at work, so she'll more than likely come during her lunch hour."

"Fair enough. Do you need anything else from me?"

"Umm... the results? Or am I pushing my luck there?"

"You are, as usual. I have another couple of PMs to perform today. I might be able to type up the reports later, it depends on how the time goes, and I have to leave early tonight. My daughter is in a school play. I promised my wife that I would attend this one as work detained me from getting to the last two. It's time I manned up and became a father as well as a pathologist. Life is passing us by so quickly, and I've decided I won't allow work to get in the way any more than necessary."

Sam put the phone on her desk and clapped, then she snatched it back up again. "Quite right, too. This last month, losing Chris the way I did, has virtually taught me the same. Sometimes it takes something as horrendous as this to ultimately change our views."

"Ah, yes, if anyone should understand my new perspective then it should definitely be you. I must get on."

She didn't get a chance to say anything else on the matter because he hung up. She should have been upset but she was used to his quirky ways. Some officers might think he was

being offhand or offensive, but not Sam. Des was one of a
kind, and there were times when she wouldn't change him
for the world and others when she could quite happily
batter him over the head with a heavy object. C'est la vie.
Sam rang Zoe back to share the news. "Zoe, it's Sam Cobbs.
How does midday sound for you to say goodbye to your
mum?"

Zoe gasped. "Today?"

"Yes. Are you up for it?"

"I suppose so. I'll need to swap my lunch hour with a
colleague, but I'm sure they won't mind, given the circumstances. Thank you so much. Is it at the hospital?"

"That's right, in Whitehaven. Hope all goes well. Don't
forget to give me a call if you need to talk to anyone."

"Thank you again, Inspector. I'll do my best not to bother
you or disrupt your investigation."

"You're welcome. Speak soon."

Sam smiled as she ended the call and left the office. She
crossed the room to chat with Claire. "How did it go with the
bank?"

"Not good. They told me they have no right to stop
people investing their own money in a company. As far as
they were concerned, the company was a genuine one on
their system at the time the transfer was made."

"Bugger. I can just imagine how that conversation went
down." She squeezed Claire's shoulder.

"Don't worry about me, boss, I can return any crap
someone in authority is willing to dish out. There was something else I noticed while I was on the phone to them."

Sam inclined her head, intrigued. "What was that?"

"At the end of her statement, I noticed a few ATM with-
drawals on the day of the victim's death. I queried it with the
bank advisor. She told me the system put a stop on her card
because it flagged up suspicious activity."

"Now that is interesting. How many are we talking about?"

"Three. All for two hundred and fifty pounds."

"You know what I'm going to ask next, don't you?"

"You want me to get in touch with the other banks involved, see if they can supply the ATM footage from the cameras on site." Claire smiled.

"Bingo. It just might be the lead we're waiting for to crack this case open. What with that and finding her phone, of course. It seems to all be slotting into place nicely. I know, maybe I shouldn't have said that out loud, it's bound to jinx us now."

CHAPTER 4

*J*im busied himself. His son was paying him a
visit that evening, and he promised to make a
concerted effort to tidy the house before he
arrived. He'd been very lax about that kind of thing lately,
after his wife's passing. He missed Annie so much. Never
dreamt that life could be this hard without his soul mate
around. Cancer sucked. She had only been fifty-eight, the
same age as he was now, when the Grim Reaper had swept
down and whisked her away from him. The illness had
lingered for two years or more, putting her through all sorts
of chemo and radiotherapy, only for it to take her from him
in the end.

He cried himself to sleep most nights, missed the feel of
her next to him. The bed seemed much colder now he was
the only one in it every night.

"Pull yourself together, man. What's done is done. Unless
you take your own life to be with her, there's nothing you or
anyone else can do to ease the pain and loneliness, although
Carl is doing his best."

His son's visits had become more frequent since his

mother's passing. He led a busy life being a long-distance lorry driver and wasn't around as much as he preferred to be, but he made up for it by visiting his father when time permitted. When he was away, his girlfriend, Yvette, popped in when she could.

He whipped around the lounge and the hallway with his trusty vacuum cleaner, thankful that he'd invested in a new one after cursing the old one for not picking up every time he used it. Now he was able to make light work of the chore he hated the most. Next, he moved into the kitchen and mopped the floor. He had trained himself to clear up the work surfaces and the draining board after every meal, that way the mess didn't overwhelm him like it used to, just after Annie had gone.

The doorbell rang. He cursed, only halfway through his task. The mop bashed against the back door. He tore through the house, wiping his hands down his trousers en route, and opened the door to find a young woman standing there.

Here goes! Yet another charity crying out for help in these troubled times we're living in.

"Can I help?"

"Mr Baldwin, I'm Jennifer Moriarty of the Cancer Trust. I was involved in your wife's care in her final days."

"Oh, you were? I thought I recognised you. What do you want?"

"A quiet word in your ear, inside if that's okay. I have some things I'd like to show you." The young woman with long brown hair draped around her shoulders held up a large cream woven bag.

"Some things? Such as?"

"Things Annie made when she was with us. I was having a tidy up the other day, and my boss suggested that I visit you, see if you wanted to keep them."

"Oh, I'm not sure how I feel about this. It's not something

I was expecting. Yes, come in. I suppose I can take a peek. Maybe my son and his girlfriend might want something as a keepsake, it depends if they're any good or not." Unexpected tears misted his vision. He stood to one side and let the woman in.

"Thanks, they're interesting, let's say that. She had so much pleasure making them while she was with us, I'm sure she would love to know they found their way back home to you and your family. In here, is it?" She pointed at the lounge door.

"That's right. You're lucky, I've just done the vacuuming, I was in the kitchen, mopping the floor, you rescued me from that overrated chore."

They both laughed, and Jim followed her into the lounge, his chest swelling with pride at how tidy it was. Had the woman shown up a few hours earlier she would have been shocked by the state the house was in.

"Won't you take a seat? I usually sit in the armchair by the fire. I'm getting on now and need the heat to prevent my veins from breaking down."

"You sit there. I'm quite warm anyway. I've been tearing around all day."

"I'm sure. I was forced to take early retirement after I had a heart attack a few years ago. Thought Annie and I would have a whale of a time being at home together after I was medically signed off, but that's when the cancer struck and took over her body."

"Oh dear, the harsh reality of life can be terrible to deal with at times. How is your health these days, Jim?"

"It was touch and go there for a while, you know, when I lost her. My heart ached for weeks. The doctor was really concerned that I might be putting it under too much strain and upped my meds again."

"How do you mend a broken heart? Not with medication,

even I know that, and I'm not medically trained. How are you now? It's been a while since she left us, hasn't it?"

"Yes, just over a year. Thirteen months, one week and six days to be precise. Not that I'm counting." Jim shrugged. "What else am I going to do with my time? I miss her every second of every waking day. You don't want to hear about my gripes, though. I'm dying to see what you have in the bag."

Jennifer beamed. Jim thought how wonderful her teeth were, white and perfectly straight, something that most people strived to achieve these days. He wondered if she'd had them professionally cleaned or whitened at the dentist or if she was just good at looking after herself in general. She had the perfect figure, her hair was long and tangle-free. Her makeup subtle, not over the top in the slightest. The type of woman he would be proud to call his daughter.

If only. I think Carl would have something to say about that after being the only child all these years.

"Let's see what we've got here." Jennifer came forward with the bag, dipped her hand inside and pulled out a hammer.

"What's that? My wife didn't make that, did she?" Jim asked, perplexed when confronted with the puzzling object.

Jennifer let out a strange laugh. "Oh no. This one I brought with me to keep you under control."

"Excuse me? What in God's name are you talking about?" Jim placed his hands on each arm of the chair and tried to ease himself out of it.

Jennifer had other ideas apparently and whacked his left hand with the hammer.

He yelled out in pain. "What the heck? You can't come into my house and treat me like this, how dare you?"

"Can't I? Are you sure about that, because I think I can. Tell me where the money is."

"What bloody money? I haven't got any." His eyes formed tiny slits, and he stared at the woman. He recognised her now but not from the cancer unit like she had said. "I know you. You wait until I see your boss. I'll be having words with him about this. Get out of my house, now!"

Jennifer laughed and brought the hammer down on his left knee. Again, Jim cried out in pain, drool dripping onto his chin.

"Get out. I won't allow you to treat me like this. I haven't got any money here."

"Ah, but we both know differently, don't we now? I'll give you one last chance to tell me before I rip this place to shreds."

"Don't do it. I've spent the day tidying up. You're going to have to believe me, there's no money in this house. I've just bought a new car, it was something I promised myself a few years ago but never got around to buying one. There was nothing left after I forked out for it. Do you have any idea how much four wheels cost to buy these days, let alone how much they are to run? The price of petrol has gone through the roof in the last year, you don't need me to tell you that, do you?"

"Shut up wittering on, old man, and hand over the money."

"For the last time, I haven't got any here. Is there something wrong with your hearing? You should get that seen to at your age, it'll only get worse the older you get."

He tried to duck as the hammer was raised. It didn't work and it came down on his temple. Instead of seeing one, as he had before, now the woman was standing before him in duplicate, heaven forbid.

"You've had your chance. You're no good to me. I'll search this shithole to find what I'm looking for, as if you can stop me from doing that."

Jim shook his head slightly, but it only made him feel ten times worse. "You're stupid if you think I would keep any money in the house." His words came out slurred; he'd surprised himself by being able to speak at all after the whack she'd given him. "Get out or I'll call the police."

"*Get out or I'll call the police,*" Jennifer mimicked, her green eyes narrowing to tiny slits as her mouth twisted.

She removed a rope from the bag she'd enticed him with upon her arrival and secured his hands in front of him. Blood dripped from the wound on his head and covered his eye. He tried to wipe it away with the sleeve of his jumper.

"Keep still, old man, or I'll make you sorry."

"You think you're so tough. Think you hold all the cards, don't ya? You don't, I know something you don't know, but you're going to find out soon enough."

Her hand shot out and clutched his throat. "Don't mess with me. Tell me what you've done. Have you hit a silent alarm or something?"

Jim stared at her, and a slight smile tugged at his mouth. "What's that saying? Ah, yes, I know something you don't know."

She glared at him and slapped his face, first one side and then the other. "You'll pay for that. You have one last chance. Either you tell me where the money is or you'll suffer the consequences."

Jim bared his teeth in a soppy grin. "My lips are sealed. Screw you, lady."

Jennifer punched him several times in the stomach, grunting through her exertion every time she struck out. "Men like you make me sick. You treat us women as the weaker sex but you haven't got a clue how much strength most of us have got in our little fingers compared to wimps like you. Now, this is the final time I'm going to ask you, where's the money?"

Determination spiked through his veins. Jim's head jutted forward, and he shouted, "I haven't got any... apart from the odd pound and scrap coins in my pocket. Why won't you believe me?"

"Because old codgers like you think you're clever and think you can get one over on us youngsters."

"Ha, call yourself young."

That offensive jibe earned Jim another punch to the stomach. "Keep it shut. If one more insult leaves your mouth..." Jennifer pulled a thumb across her throat. "I'll kill you. And do you know what? I'll bloody enjoy it as well. Men like you deserve to be put in their place."

"Bring it on. I'm strong, I can handle anything you're willing to dish out. The sooner I meet up with Annie the better, so do your bloody worst. If you've got the guts."

Jennifer's hand disappeared into the bag, and she withdrew a large kitchen knife. Jim's gaze was drawn to the blade which glistened in the light overhead.

"You were saying?"

"That I don't give two hoots what you do to me. I will die having the knowledge that you'll get caught as you leave this house." He watched the confusion etch into her features.

"Meaning what?"

He remained tight-lipped and smiled. Testing whether she had the guts to follow through or not. "I know something you don't know." He said the sentence in a singsong, childlike voice which appeared to only infuriate her further.

She took a step closer, her gaze locked on to his, and this time, instead of using her fist, she stabbed him in the stomach. His eyes widened as the realisation dawned.

"You bitch!"

She grinned and nodded. "There's more where that came from, old man. Now that you know I mean business, why don't you tell me where the money is?"

His eyes fluttered shut with the pain then sprang open again, the defiance manifesting there. "Go fuck yourself."

Jennifer growled and stabbed him several times until that defiance dispersed, along with his last breath.

JENNIFER STARED down at Jim's helpless body. "You're a fool, old man. Things might have turned out differently, if only you had saved me the bother of searching for what I know is hidden here. Now I have to waste more of my precious time, hunting in every nook and damn cranny to find the money." She sensed Jim's spirit lingering, probably laughing at her. She couldn't have that, so she plunged the knife into his chest and dragged it out again. The gesture zapped her of what little strength she had left after her exertions. Tired of looking at him, she ran upstairs to begin her search, snapping on a pair of latex gloves as she walked. She pulled out every drawer, tossing aside the clothes in each one, but found nothing.

Her frustrations inched up to another level before she moved over to the wardrobe. The man's clothes reminded her of what her elderly grandfather used to parade around in. She loved him dearly at the beginning, that was, until his true colours had shown. He had helped bring her up when her own parents had died in a rail crash over thirty years ago while they were on a trip to London.

Jennifer shoved the untimely sentimental thoughts aside to concentrate on the task in hand. Another thorough sift through the contents came up blank. Slamming the doors shut, she stood back and glanced around the room. This time her gaze landed on the plastic boxes on top of the old wardrobe. *How did I miss those before?* Being quite short, she looked around for a chair or something that would take her weight, enabling her to carry out the search. A rickety old chair tucked in the corner would have to do.

Tentatively, she climbed onto the seat and grabbed the lip of the plastic box. It was too high for her to carry out the search up there, so she eased it down the side of the wardrobe, keeping her balance by holding the back of the chair with her other hand. Once they were both on the floor, she tore off the lid and tossed things aside until she found what she was searching for. A notebook with all his passwords clearly laid out sitting alongside several debit cards from different banks. After tucking all the contents into her bag, she ran back down the stairs, pausing in the lounge to check the old man hadn't miraculously come back to life. He hadn't. She removed all the evidence that she had been there and left via the front door, aware the darkness of the evening would cloak her departure.

She slammed the front door shut behind her. This was echoed by the sound of a car door being closed near to the house. Her heart rate escalated, and she scurried up the short drive where she bumped into a younger man. "Sorry, my fault."

"That's okay. I should have been looking where I was going. Have you been to visit my father?"

"Yes. I'm running late for my next appointment. Nice meeting you. I've left him in good spirits in there." She suppressed the smile threatening to emerge and the laugh tickling her throat.

"That's Dad for you. Always got a cheerful disposition. Nice to meet you. Enjoy the rest of your evening, hope it's not all work and you manage to find some time to relax at the end of it."

"Don't worry. I will. Goodbye." Head down, she crossed the road and got in her car. She was undecided whether to take the risk or not. Peering over her shoulder, she saw him still watching her and had to fight the temptation to remove the knife from her bag and return to finish him off, sending him on his way to meet his father. She decided against it and took the risk of just driving off. She even waved as she drove past the young man staring after her.

Shit, he's going to take down my numberplate now. Not ideal. Never mind, I'll find a way around it, I always do.

CHAPTER 5

*S*am was on her way home when the call came in. She and the team had decided to work an extra hour or so that evening, not wishing to put off some of the leads they had gathered until the day after.

"DI Sam Cobbs. How can I help?"

"Glad I caught you, ma'am. We've received a call regarding a suspicious death and thought you'd be able to attend the scene," the woman on control stated.

"Why me? My shift should have ended a while ago. I'm late going home as it is. Are you sure there's no one else available?"

"There isn't, ma'am, believe me, I've tried."

Sam indicated and drew the car into a lay-by. Sighing, she said, "You'd better give me the details then."

"Thank you. It's eighty-nine Stolkey Road, that's over in Stainburn."

"You're kidding me, that's on the other side of the town. Okay, ignore me. I'll use the siren. What will I find when I get there?"

"A man in his late fifties, stabbed to death in his own home."

"Crap. Thanks, I'm on my way. Is everyone else on call-outs or what?"

"There are a few meetings going on, and yes, a couple are attending a few accident scenes. Sorry to disturb your evening, but I appreciate you responding to the call. Not sure I would have, in your shoes."

"We do what we can to assist the general public, even when we're off duty, right?"

"If you say so, ma'am. Thank you again for attending."

"I won't say it's a pleasure." Sam laughed and ended the call. She flicked the switch on her siren, and the blue lights lit up the area around her. There wasn't much traffic where she currently was, but it got worse the closer she got to the centre. Thankfully, there were no stubborn idiots on the road. That could often be an issue in emergencies, dealing with imbeciles who refused to pull over to let an emergency vehicle pass.

Sam arrived at the location around ten minutes later, half the time it would have taken her if she hadn't resorted to using the siren, an added bonus to having them on board, not that she would ever use them to wade through the traffic if she was off duty, unlike other officers she could mention.

Des and his techs were already at the scene.

Sam trotted up to his van the second she laid eyes on him. "Evening, Des, got a suit I can pinch, have you?"

"Always on the cadge, ain't ya? There, on the left. I wasn't expecting to see you at this time of night, don't you have a home to go to?"

"I was on my way when the call came in. I could fire that one back at you. Wait, how did your daughter's evening go?"

"It went. The less said about it the better. Not my type of thing at all. The things we do to appease our families."

"You're a miserable old sod."

"I'm not denying it either. Back to work, eh?"

Sam slid the suit out of the plastic sleeve and slipped into it, then she hunted for a pair of shoe covers which Des located for her on his side of the van. "What have we got?"

"Man in his late fifties, stabbed to death. His son found him at just after six-thirty. He dropped by after work as arranged and found his father unresponsive, dead in other words."

"Yeah, I figured you meant that. How many times was the victim stabbed?"

"Too many to count at the moment. Overkill definitely."

"Any sign of a break-in?" Sam glanced at the house and the situation it was in on the estate. There were a few streetlights around but nothing close to the residence in question.

"None that we can find."

"Where's his son?"

"I asked him to sit in his car, rather than contaminate the crime scene further. He's in a state of shock."

"I'd be surprised if he wasn't. I'll have a chat with him in a second or two. All right if I come in and have a snoop around first?"

"Sure, fine by me. Just don't get under my feet, you know I can't stand it."

Sam rolled her eyes. "As if I would. Have your guys had a chance to search the rest of the house?"

"Yes, the bedroom is a tip. It would appear the murderer was searching for something. There's a plastic box on the bedroom floor, the lid is off. I'm assuming the killer found what they were looking for and left. Umm... I should have mentioned this before, my bad. The son bumped into a woman on the path, she was just leaving his father's house."

"What? What's wrong with you? Of course I'd need that

piece of information right away." Sam stripped off her suit again.

"What are you doing?" Des asked, puzzled.

"I need to see what the son has to say. Having a nose around the crime scene can wait on this occasion."

"Whatever. He's sitting in the red SUV." Des pointed across the road.

"I'll be back soon."

"See you inside. Good luck. I hope he makes sense, because he wasn't before."

"Great. I'll see soon enough." Sam left Des tinkering with his equipment and crossed the road to the son's car. She tapped on the window and held up her ID card. "I'm DI Sam Cobbs. Can I have a quick word?"

The man lowered his window. "Carl Baldwin. My father has been killed."

A drop of rain landed on her nose. "Shall we talk inside? I can jump in beside you."

"Yes, please do." He glanced over his shoulder at the house.

Sam smiled and ran around the front of the car. She removed her notebook from her jacket pocket and jumped in beside him. "I'm so sorry for your loss, Carl. Finding your father like that must have come as a great shock."

"It did. We were really close. Mum only died last year... we'd become closer still after we lost her... and now this. What am I going to do now? Burying my mother ripped me to shreds, and now I've got to go through all that shit again, laying him to rest. How is that fair? Both parents gone within a year of each other."

Sam placed a hand on his forearm. "I can't even begin to imagine how awful that must be to cope with. Are you up to telling me what happened when you got here this evening?"

He shrugged. "Why not? It's not like there's anything else

going on in my mind right now. That woman. I'll never forget her face."

Sam's intrigue crept up a couple of levels. "You saw her, close up?"

"Oh, yes. She stood there, smiling at me, holding a damn conversation with me. I even waved her off. What a frigging fool I was."

"She showed no signs of discomfort or even remorse?"

"None whatsoever. She was chatting to me as if nothing had bloody happened. She can't be all there, can she? To kill my father like that and then just walk away, chatting to me as if nothing had happened." He shook his head and sighed. "Why? Dad has never harmed anyone in his life. Why enter his house and take him out in such a callous way? That's what I'm struggling to get my head around."

"That's understandable. Can you describe this woman for me?"

"Gosh, now you're asking. I'm ashamed to say that I found her attractive, maybe that's what she latched on to and why she didn't show any sign of wanting to abscond."

"Don't beat yourself up about it. Killers are in a league of their own, they come in all shapes and sizes and take pleasure in toying with folks. Was she tall or short?"

"Quite short, around five two or three. Really long hair that draped over her shoulders at the front, on either side. It was too dark to see what colour it was or what colour her eyes were. Sorry, I'm hopeless, I know."

"You're not, stop thinking that way. You're in shock. I'd be the same if I'd just walked in and found my father dead. Did you make out any distinguishing features to this woman?"

"The thing that struck me the most was her perfect smile. The straightest white teeth I've ever seen."

"Probably had constructive surgery on them. See, you're doing well, that's a great snippet to share. Was she slim?"

"Yes, very. She wore quite flat heels. Had on a dark coat and trousers, I think, although that part is a bit sketchy."

"Again, that's excellent. Which way did she head off?"

"That way. She jumped into a car similar to this one, not sure of the make or model, but it was light in colour, possibly silver."

"A silver SUV. I don't suppose you took note of the number, did you?"

"I didn't. She drew my attention but not the car as such. Hang on. There was a GH in the plate somewhere."

"Great stuff. See, you're really good at this, under the circumstances."

"I want to help in any way I can. She has to be caught. There was no reason for her to kill my father, none at all. I still can't believe it. She was there, standing in front of me, holding a conversation as if everything was all right. How sick and deranged is that? If I ever lay eyes on her again... well, one of us won't come out of the meeting alive, I can tell you that."

"Hopefully it won't come to that. You've given me enough to make a difference, to do all I can to track her down. Can you recall ever seeing the woman before? Does your father have many visitors come to the house?"

"No, I think I would have remembered coming across her over the years, and no, Dad didn't have that many visitors, just me really. He doesn't have any siblings, and his parents died long ago."

"Did he mention in passing that he was expecting someone to pop around and see him?"

"No, not at all. He knew I was dropping in this evening, I think he would have tried to put me off had he known that this woman was paying a visit."

"Has your father had any concerns lately?"

He faced her and frowned. "Such as?"

"Any problems with finances or health issues for instance?"

"No, he was in good health, well, except for his heart problem. He was forced to retire a few years ago. He's been under the specialist ever since, for all the good it did him, in the end. Jesus, he's fought so hard to stay with us, especially after going through the trauma of losing Mum, only to go out like this. Life is so cruel, wicked and unfair."

"We'll get the person responsible for this. I promise I won't rest until she's banged up."

"Thank you. I hope they're not just words, it's easy to pacify folks when they are grieving."

"I don't work that way, I swear. Is there anything else you can tell me?"

"No, I think I've told you everything I can remember. What happens now?"

"The Forensic team will spend the next couple of days at the house, assessing the scene and taking any evidence samples they find in the different rooms in the house. One thing I need to mention is that the pathologist told me, when I arrived, that the killer might have been searching for something in the bedroom. Any idea what that might be?"

"In the bedroom? Where?"

"He said something about a plastic box being on the floor. Do you know what your father kept in the box?"

Carl stared off in the distance as he thought. "Paperwork? I'm really not sure. It's not something we had ever discussed, but it seems likely, doesn't it?"

"Maybe. I'm going to enter the house now and see for myself."

"No chance I can come with you, I take it?"

"Sorry, no. The house will be off limits to everyone except the techs for at least two to three days. They need to be thorough, I'm sure you can understand that."

"I do. I feel so inadequate, even more so than when I found him. I never thought I'd be ringing nine-nine-nine so soon after losing my mother and definitely not in these circumstances."

Sam clutched his forearm. "Is there anyone else I can ring, ask them to come and collect you rather than you drive away from here under your own steam?"

"No, I'll be all right. Or maybe I'll never be all right again in the future, I don't know. Seeing him like that, a bloody mess, has knocked the wind out of my sails. I've always considered myself a strong character, but this situation is really testing me, I can tell you."

"It's bound to have an impact. Don't punish yourself and think you're a failure, you're not. If you're sure you're going to be all right, you're free to go when you want."

"Thank you, for all you've done. I like you, Inspector. I feel confident that you will find this woman and punish her for robbing me of my beloved father."

"I won't let you down, you have my word on that."

He gave her his details and Sam left the car. She stood on the pavement and watched him drive away before she returned to Des's van to retrieve her white paper suit and shoe coverings. She paused at the cordon to sign the log and entered the house. "Where are you, Des?"

"In the first room on the right."

Sam followed his instructions and paused in the doorway to assess the scene for a second or two. Then she moved closer.

"He doesn't bite, he's dead!" Des quipped.

"Not funny, and a joke in very poor taste, I might add."

"I knew you had lost your sense of humour, thanks for proving it."

"What a mess. I'm not surprised the son was shaken up

after finding his father like this. Any evidence lying around, or are we talking about a pro here?"

"Too early to tell. Personally, I haven't found anything yet, but then, I have been otherwise engaged."

"Can I take a look around?"

"As long as you've got the necessary protection on, then yes, please do."

"I'll get back to you soon." She left the room and wandered up the hallway into the kitchen.

The back door was locked; there was a mop and bucket in the otherwise tidy room. *At least he cared enough about his property to keep it clean, unlike most men I've come across on my numerous callouts.* Retracing her steps, she passed the lounge on her way up the stairs to the main bedroom. That's where she found the plastic box and the wardrobe doors and the drawers all open. The bed was made, so her first assumption was that the room was generally kept tidy and that the killer had been searching for something, but what? The second murder this week where personal belongings had been tampered with. Why?

She got down on her knees and sifted through the paperwork. The victim's marriage and birth certificates were both there, along with a copy of his driving licence. His passport was visible at the bottom, through the plastic. A burglar would take those, maybe for ID fraud or to sell on the black market. What specifically were they after? It was a perplexing situation for Sam, one that she would run past the team in the morning.

Sam ventured downstairs again and into the lounge.

"You were quick, did you find what you were looking for?" Des asked.

"The killer was searching for something specific. I'm at a loss as to what that was at this point. Personal paperwork that would cause his murder, it doesn't ring true, does it?"

"It does seem odd. Did you get much out of the son?"

"Only that he lost his mother last year and now his father has been taken from him. He did mention the woman, feels guilty for taking an interest in her, if she was indeed the killer, and there's no reason for either of us to think otherwise if she was caught leaving his house."

"It's all very strange. He needn't feel guilty, we all know what killers can get up to when they need to cover their tracks or, as in this case, to divert suspicion."

"I'm going to flood the area with uniforms, strike while the iron is hot on this one, see if any of the neighbours either saw this woman arrive or leave."

"Sounds like a good idea. In the meantime, we'll do all we can for the poor bugger here before we move him to the mortuary."

"I told the son the house would be out of bounds for a couple of days. He agreed not to come back too soon."

"Good. Let's hope the guys can find us a few clues to go on, eh?"

"Yeah, one question: are we linking the crimes? I mean, it would make sense to me."

"Then yes, I was in two minds about it, but now that you've raised the subject, why don't we go ahead and link them?"

Sam smiled and left him to it. She stepped outside and rang the station. The evening desk sergeant answered her call. He listened to her request and assured her his team would be with her within fifteen minutes. Sam hung up. Instead of going back to her car, she decided to have a word with the neighbours to the right.

Holding up her warrant card, she smiled at the elderly woman as she opened the door. "Hi, I'm DI Sam Cobbs. I'm investigating a crime that was committed next door."

The woman tucked herself behind the door. "He's dead,

isn't he? Otherwise, you lot wouldn't be here en masse, would you?"

Sam nodded. "Sorry, yes. Did you know your neighbour well?"

"Well enough. His wife used to run errands for me during the winter when I was unable to get out. Jim was a treasure, he tried to help me out with a couple of DIY jobs that were driving me nuts, but although he had a go, he always managed to make things a lot worse, bless him. Hush my mouth for speaking badly of the dead, I didn't mean anything nasty by that, I swear."

"Please, don't concern yourself about that. I'm sorry for the loss of your friend. Our aim now is to do our very best to catch his killer. Can you tell me if you saw anything earlier? I should make that clearer for you: did you see anyone enter Jim's garden earlier this evening?"

"No, I can't say I did. I moved my lounge to the back a few years ago because we get more sun out there and it warms the house up, so I don't have to put the heating on."

"Sounds a sensible idea. What are the walls like? Did you hear anything going on next door?"

"No. I wear a hearing aid most of the time. It works now and again, but I usually keep the TV up loud so I can hear what the people are saying. I'm not one for lip reading, not these days, not with my poor eyesight as well. Hey, what am I saying? You don't want to hear about all my ailments, you're here on important business. Maybe it's the shock talking." She finally moved out from behind the door.

Sam could see how visibly frail she was. Her arms were skinny, her neck long and slender.

"I'm sorry you're not too well."

"It's not that I'm not well, my body is deteriorating quicker than I expected. I'm only eighty-six. Still, I'm going to outlive poor Jim. What a dreadful few years he's had, what with his heart problem and then Annie passing away like she did. Poor Carl, I saw him sitting in his car out there when all the noise was going on, your lot arriving et cetera. I happened to be putting my bin out, otherwise I wouldn't have heard a thing out the back. Was he all right? Carl, I mean?"

"Yes, upset and devastated, obviously, but I'm sure he'll bounce back once he's had time to reflect. Okay, if you didn't see or hear anything then I'd better move on to the other neighbours. Please, take care of yourself, won't you?"

"I'll do my best. I have a carer who drops by in the morning and the evening, you know, to get me up and put me to bed. Most of the time I manage on my own."

"Glad you're being well looked after." Sam smiled and turned to walk away.

"Thank you, dear. Do your very best for old Jim, don't let his death become a statistic only."

"I won't. I promise."

She waited while the woman closed the door and then moved on to the house on the other side. This time a man in his early forties opened the door, a frown creasing his forehead where the hair was receding.

Sam flashed her ID and introduced herself. "Sorry to trouble you. I'm investigating an incident that took place next door earlier this evening and I wondered if you perhaps either saw or heard anything."

"Ah, I thought you might come knocking, eventually. Yes, I heard Jim cry out several times." He sighed and shrugged. "I never thought anything of it at the time. You know, presumed he was doing some sort of DIY and had hit his hand a couple of times with the hammer, that sort of thing. I do it all the time."

"Sadly, that wasn't the case at all. Around what time was this?"

"Now you're asking. I suppose the news was on, so it must have been between six and six-thirty."

Sam noted the times down. "Did you see anyone arrive?"

"There was a woman hanging around. I came home about five-thirty, maybe five minutes later, and she was here then. She was sitting in a silver Kia."

"That's brilliant. I knew it was a silver SUV, but now you've given me the make it's going to be a lot easier to find. I don't suppose you took note of the number, did you?"

"Sorry, I didn't see any need for it. Don't tell me she did the deed on old Jim, did she?"

Sam shrugged. "It seems that way. Jim's son bumped into her leaving the house when he arrived."

"Shit! Seriously? He came face to face with his own father's killer and let her get away? Sorry, that was unfair. That's going to bloody play on his mind for years to come, right?"

"You're not wrong. Some killers have no shame, it's all part of their performance, adding a hint of danger to their game."

"Despicable. Do you know why he was killed?"

"Not yet, no. Have you seen this woman hanging around here before?"

"No, tonight was the first time. You think Jim was targeted specifically?"

"We're not sure at present, it's still too early to either suggest that or rule it out completely. Did you know Jim well?"

"We've seen each other down at the pub and had a natter over a pint or two, nothing more than that. Although he did ask me to lend him a hand shifting some furniture around last year, after his wife died. It was when Carl, his son, was on holiday. I willingly volunteered. If you can't help out your neighbours, it's a poor tale, isn't it?"

Sam smiled. "Indeed. There are not many kind-spirited people around these days. No, let me correct that statement, I think doing good deeds for people has improved since the lockdown days."

"Yeah, I agree. That horrible time in our lives changed a lot of people's perspectives, I suppose. Shame it didn't have the same effect on the killers in our society, eh?"

"It is. Is there anything else you can tell me about this woman or the vehicle?"

"No. I don't think so, except she didn't look like a killer. Not that they walk around with a neon sign over their heads or anything."

"I wish they did, it would make my job a lot easier to contend with. Thanks for your help. Would it be all right if you provided us with a statement as to what you heard and saw this evening?"

"Of course. Tonight?"

"I can arrange that. The place is going to be flooded with uniformed officers soon. I'll get one to drop by and see you."

"Fine by me. Good luck with your investigation. I have to ask, do you think the rest of us are in any danger?"

"Honestly, I don't think so. But it might be an idea to be more vigilant over the next few days, just in case."

"She wouldn't take the risk of coming back here, would she?"

"Who knows? Killers can be a law unto themselves, until they're caught."

"Hopefully that will be sooner rather than later, eh?"

"That's the plan. Take care."

Sam walked back up the path and glanced up to see four patrol cars pulling into the road. She was glad the desk sergeant had kept to his word and sent enough reinforcements to take over from her. She waited on the pavement for the officers to gather around and explained what she needed to happen, then she sent them on their way.

With everything organised, a wave of exhaustion overwhelmed her, and Sam jumped back in the car and headed home. She rang Doreen on the way. "Hi, it's me. Sorry for messing you about today, Doreen. I'm on my way now."

"You haven't, don't worry. Anyway, Sonny has gone for a walk with Rhys."

"He has? That's… unusual."

"I thought the same. Did I do the right thing, letting him take Sonny?"

"Oh, yes. No, it was just me thinking out loud. He'll be fine, Rhys would never hurt him. I'll see you soon."

"Good, I would hate to do anything that might upset you, Sam."

"You could never do that. I won't be long."

She ended the call and put her foot down. After the way Rhys had reacted at the park the last time they were there, bad thoughts plagued her mind on the journey home. She tried several dismal attempts to push them aside only for them to return with a vengeance.

Sam arrived home at nearly nine to see Rhys with Sonny trotting happily alongside him. Her heart gladdened at the sight of them together. She had a stern word with herself for adding the unnecessary burden of worry to her day.

Rhys opened the car door and gave her a kiss when she got out. She ruffled Sonny's head and smiled. "Been out on a jaunt, have we?"

"I didn't know how long you were going to be. I arrived home late and thought Sonny would need his walk, so I dived right in without thinking."

"Without thinking?" Sam queried.

"After what happened the other night. Me melting down like that. It's true what they say, you need to get back on that horse again if you're determined to get over an unwanted obstacle standing in your way. Sonny helped me to achieve that tonight."

"You went back to the park?"

"Correction. I didn't have a choice, Sonny dragged me into the park. There I combatted my fears. He's an amazing dog, it's as if he knew I had struggled the other night."

"You're the amazing one. I'm so proud of you. So glad you had a breakthrough, that park means a lot to both of us."

"It sure does. Enough of this. Are you hungry?"

"Am I? My stomach stopped rumbling hours ago, it's given up on getting fed this evening. I'm sure once I latch on to a fantastic aroma filling the kitchen, it'll welcome food with open arms. What did you have in mind?"

"Depends on what you have in the fridge. I could knock up one of my special frittatas, if you're interested?"

"I am. We could both prepare the veggies, that way it'll be ready sooner."

"Sounds good to me. You sort Sonny out first. I'm sure he's run off some extra calories down at the park."

"Did you let him off the lead?" she asked, doing her best to hide the panic nibbling at her insides.

"Yes. His recall was excellent. He's a well-behaved dog. That shouldn't come as a surprise to you."

"He's adorable." She wanted to add something more about Benji being fabulous, too, but decided to leave it there.

Together they prepared the meal, and then, over dinner, Rhys spoke in general about the clients he had seen during the day.

"I don't know how you do it. Offer advice to all and sundry, different advice to the individuals who are going through such diverse situations."

"It's all down to my training. We're taught to assess individuals' needs. There's no real magic solution, you know, one size fits all to everyone's problems. Enough about me, how did your day go? Why were you so late?"

"It was a hectic day. I was heading home when I received a call to attend another murder scene. Get this, the killer was seen by the victim's son. I can't imagine what an horrendous ordeal that must have been for him and what kind of torment he's going to put himself through over the coming days."

"Damn. That's tough to deal with. I don't often say this, but maybe you should give him one of my cards. I wouldn't charge him for his treatment, so I wouldn't be touting for business."

"You would do that? For me? For Carl?"

"Of course. He'll be going through all sorts of inner turmoil, dealing with his father's death, with the added stress of knowing that he confronted the killer... blimey, it doesn't bear thinking about, does it? Yes, I'd be more than willing to help ease him through this troubled time."

"I'm so lucky to have a genuinely nice man in my life. Willing to give up your time in this way... it blows me away."

"Nonsense. I'm sure many of my colleagues would do the same if a similar situation cropped up in their area."

"I beg to differ. It takes a compassionate man to go the extra mile to help someone get over their grief." She leaned over and kissed him.

Sonny moaned under the table, and they both laughed.

"Oi, you, stop being jealous. You've had your share of fuss this evening, now it's my turn."

"Why don't we do the dishes together and see what films are on the box?"

Sam ran her hand around his handsome face and smiled. "I've got a better idea, and it involves us transferring upstairs, not into the lounge."

Rhys's eyes widened. "You don't say. Are you going to give me a hint?"

"Well, if I have to do that then my powers of seduction must be lacking, big time."

They cleared the table together. Rhys started on the washing-up and Sam saw to Sonny's needs. She let him in the garden only to find it had started raining again.

"Typical for this time of year. Roll on spring, it can't come soon enough for me."

"I think we should book a holiday, what do you say? My treat," Rhys announced.

"What? I can't let you do that. I'm due some time off in March. Oh my, a holiday... I can't remember the last time I actually took off somewhere, except with you, for the odd weekend to a cottage with Sonny... and Benji," she mumbled the dead dog's name.

"Stop that... we should be allowed to talk about him without any recriminations. We need to get over this. He's gone, there's no point in either of us dwelling on it. He will never be forgotten or replaced, just like Sonny could never be replaced."

Sam took three paces and ended up in his arms. She rested her head against his chest and listened to his heart beating. It was such a comfort to hold him so close once more. She was determined to never let him leave again, but was it too soon to push their relationship to another level? She leaned back, and their gazes met.

"Is it time?"

"Time? For what?" There was that twinkle in his eyes again.

She slapped his chest. "Stop teasing me. Are you telling me that you think it's time we moved on? Started over? That you're ready to forgive me?"

Rhys placed a finger under her chin, and their lips met.

When they parted, he whispered, "Let's get one thing straight, there's nothing to forgive. You weren't at fault, it was me, I overreacted to the situation."

She shook her head and placed a finger on his lips to silence him. "You didn't. I would have reacted in exactly the same way if Sonny… had passed away in that fatal accident. There was only one person to blame for what happened that night, and he's no longer with us. They're right, the experts and non-experts alike who always preach that suicide is a coward's way out."

It was Rhys's turn to shake his head. "I've never believed or understood why someone should say that. Ending one's own life takes a heap of courage in my opinion. Chris wanted to literally go out with a bang, whether it was his intention to cause the devastation he did is another matter entirely. I understand his reasons, though. He wanted you back, and you rejected him."

"He had his chance with me. I clearly wasn't enough for him, otherwise he wouldn't have ended up in another woman's bed."

"I guess. No matter how many times we go over this, try to analyse it, it's not going to change the outcome, therefore, I suggest we move on with our lives."

Sam inclined her head to the right. "Meaning?"

"Meaning that I think we should pick up where we left off and I should move in here and help you with the bills."

Her heart melted. "Are you sure? The last thing I want to do is put you under any kind of pressure."

"How will you be doing that, if this is my suggestion?"

They sealed the deal with a kiss and retired to the bedroom to discuss it further.

CHAPTER 6

The next morning, Sam was up with the birds. Sonny had been walked and deposited next door to Doreen, she'd kissed Rhys farewell for the day and was now driving into work. Her mind was in a vortex of confusion about the cases she and the team were dealing with at present.

They have to be linked. Are we looking at a female serial killer here? She seems too perfect by what Carl had to say about her. Maybe she's a man dressed as a woman to try and fool us. That's not unheard of, I've definitely come across something of that nature in the past. Not often, granted. But if there's a means to an end, a killer will go above and beyond to achieve their aims, won't they?

She pulled into the space next to her partner and turned to wave. He seemed distracted by something. It wasn't until she got out of her car and peered through the window that she realised Bob was messing about with his mobile. Sam knocked on the window. The mobile shot out of his hands, and he glared at her.

She gave him a toothy grin and mouthed, "Morning,

lovely day." Not sure who she was trying to kid as it was raining cats and dogs at that moment.

Bob's mouth moved, but Sam had trouble deciphering what he said, although it didn't take her long to figure out what it was likely to be. She stepped back to shelter under the slight canopy, the extended roofline the station had to offer, and watched Bob retrieve his phone from the footwell and then get out of his vehicle.

"There should be a law against that," he grumbled.

Sam caught up with him and nudged him with her elbow. "Against what?"

"You creeping up on people."

She laughed. He opened the door to the station and motioned for her to go first, if a tad grudgingly.

"I didn't," she said. "What were you up to? Doing something you shouldn't have been doing, no doubt."

"That's where you're wrong. I was checking my emails. The car insurance is due, and I was waiting for the quote to come through."

Sam raised an eyebrow as if he had made that up to deceive her.

He tutted. "I couldn't give a toss if you believe me or not, it happens to be the truth." With that, his phone announced the arrival of a message or email. He stared at the screen and then showed her.

"All right, I believe you. What's up with you being so touchy first thing?"

"I'm not."

"You could have fooled me. Lighten up, man. Hey, we've got a long day ahead of us."

He frowned. "How come?"

"I'll tell you along with the rest of the team."

"Secrets, secrets, that's all you seem to thrive on lately."

Sam laughed. "What the hell are you talking about?"

Bob punched his number into the security pad, and the door sprang open. "Nothing. Just saying… that once upon a time you used to open up to me more."

"Sorry, I don't remember such times. May I remind you that I'm your senior officer, partner?"

"Ooo… get you, ramming it down my throat."

"Christ, you really did get out of the wrong side of the bed this morning, didn't you?"

He mumbled an apology and pushed open the door to the incident room. They were the first to arrive.

"You get the coffees, and I'll fire up the computers then check what awaits me on my desk," Sam said.

"Whatever, suits me."

After seeing the pile of brown envelopes and checking the number of emails awaiting her, she returned to the incident room and decided to bring the whiteboard up to date with the details of the latest victim.

"What? There's been another murder? Why didn't you tell me? Ring me if you attended the scene?" Bob said.

She faced him. "Are you kidding me? Have you seen the bloody mood you're in this morning? I fear I would have been subjected to a lot worse had I rung you to attend the incident with me last night. I received the call on the way home, at around seven. Anyway, I'd rather wait until the others arrive before I reveal what happened. Gone are the days when I repeat myself over and over, life's too short as it is."

Bob muttered something and turned his head the other way.

Claire entered the room which put a halt to Sam challenging him, not for the first time that morning.

"Morning, Claire. How are you today?"

Claire's gaze shot between Sam and Bob before landing back on Sam. "Yeah, fine today, boss. You?"

"Oh, yes, we're all tickety-boo, aren't we, Bob?"

He rolled his eyes and crossed his arms. "Yes, all fine and dandy."

"Grab yourself a drink, Claire. We'll wait for the others to show up and then get cracking."

Claire's gaze was drawn to the board. "Not another one?"

Sam nodded. "I'll fill in the details soon."

"Yeah, she hasn't even told me, Claire," Bob said grumpily.

"I'm sure the boss has her reasons. Anyone want another drink?"

"No, we're fine," Sam replied for both of them.

Bob shot her another disdainful look. She smiled and got back to bringing the board up to date. The rest of the team filed into the room in dribs and drabs. At two minutes to nine, Sam brought everyone's attention to the board, which she had now completed.

"Right, this is what I had to deal with on the way home last night. I sense a long day ahead of us, folks, so listen up. I'm going to start off by saying that there is a distinct possibility that there is a connection between this murder and the case we already have the pleasure of working on."

"How can you tell, when we have very little evidence to go by with the Callard case?" Bob asked the most obvious question.

"All right, at the moment I'm calling it a loose connection. At both scenes the victim's personal paperwork was sifted through. Who's to say what was missing from both locations?"

"That's it?" Bob queried. He folded his arms and shook his head.

"While I'm willing to admit it's not much, it's also something I'm not willing to dismiss either. Therefore, this morning, I want us all to put as much effort into finding a possible link between the two victims, Tammy Callard and Jim Baldwin, as we can."

"Simples, right?" Bob asked.

"Not necessarily, no. Let's not put obstacles in the way, Bob, eh? Work with me on this one, just this once, okay?"

Bob raised his hands. "If that's what you want. As a team we'll do our very best to find a link, you know we will. You're going to need to give us some insight into what we're dealing with in order for that to go ahead, though."

"If you'll give me a chance, that's what I intend to do right now, DS Jones."

Bob's face flushed under her glare.

"As I was saying, I was called out to a murder scene last night. When I got there, I found the victim had been stabbed numerous times. He'd also been hit with a blunt object, probably something along the lines of a hammer."

"How old was the victim? Was he too old to defend himself?" Bob asked.

"Late fifties to early sixties. His son was at the scene. He told me his father was in relatively good health although he had to retire early a few years ago due to heart problems. Carl, the son, also revealed that his mother had died last year as well."

"What a shame, to lose your parents within a year of each other," Suzanna said.

Sam nodded. "I agree. Here's the most surprising thing about what occurred last night: when Carl showed up at the house—it was an arranged visit to see his father—the killer was leaving his father's property. They bumped into each other in the front garden."

Fully alert at this news, Bob sat upright and asked, "What? Did he tackle the killer?"

"No. He was a little embarrassed about the incident."

Bob opened his mouth to say something else, but Sam silenced him with her raised hand.

"I'll get the story told with fewer interruptions."

"Sorry."

"What we do have is a description of the killer and the vehicle she left the scene in."

"Wow, have you circulated the details?" Bob asked.

"Of course. I need to check with the front desk to see if anything has come of that yet. I also rallied the troops and got them knocking on the other houses in the street, while it was still early enough to do so. I've yet to chase up the results of their actions. I'll do that after our meeting. What concerns me is the blatant front the killer had, talking to Carl, as if nothing had happened. He understandably feels mortified by this, and I suspect it will only add to his anguish and disbelief in losing his father."

"That's terrible," Claire said. "I can understand him feeling that way, but he really shouldn't. If they bumped into each other outside the property and Carl wasn't aware of what had gone on inside, how can he blame himself?"

"I agree. What we need to do is try and track down this vehicle. According to Carl, the plate included a GH. That shouldn't be difficult to trace, should it? One of the neighbours told me he thought the car was a silver Kia. Until then, we knew it was a silver SUV."

Claire tapped at her keyboard. "Leave it with me."

"I was hoping you'd volunteer, Claire."

Liam raised a tentative hand. "Dare I say that I seem to remember seeing a silver SUV outside the garage the night Tammy was killed?"

"Check it out, Liam, we need to be sure. If you're right, then we're definitely travelling along the right lines. So, to sum up, our main aim today is to see if there were any major links between the victims, if only to prevent another murder falling into our laps. We need to trace the car. Do the necessary background checks, i.e. financial and social media, although I'm not sure the latter will help as both the victims were older." Sam cringed. "Forget I said that, I shouldn't class being in one's fifties as being old these days."

"Maybe fifty years ago, yeah, definitely not these days," Bob agreed. "Are you going to give us a description of the female? We might be able to spot her on the database, if someone is given the task of trawling through it."

"She had long dark hair. Carl wasn't sure what colour eyes she had because it was dark around that time. Slim build. Her teeth were perfect, straight and white."

Bob frowned. "And that's it?"

"She was quite short too. It's better than nothing, Bob. Stop putting obstructions in the way, it's not nice and it's not clever."

He folded his arms, and his chin rested on his chest.

Great, now he's sulking. "Anything else? No? Right, then let's get cracking, team." She turned on her heel and tore into her office, closing the door behind her. After taking in the distant view of the hills to calm her spiking heart rate, she sat behind her desk and rang the desk sergeant. "Nick, it's Sam Cobbs. Sorry I didn't stop for a chat on the way in, I had other things on my mind."

"I could see that, ma'am, no problem. Do you want to know how it went last night?"

"Yes. Did anything surface?"

"Sort of. One of the neighbours was pulling up as the woman left the road. He had a dashcam and caught a good image of her number plate. I've since run it through the system and..."

"Don't tell me, the car was stolen?"

"Correct, or the number plate was. It should be sitting on a Ford Ka right now."

"Shit! I had a feeling that might be the case. This woman is a bloody professional, she's got everything covered, or so it would seem. I don't suppose the dashcam came up with a good image of the driver, did it?"

"Sorry to disappoint you, no, it didn't."

"Great. Did your guys manage to obtain any further information from the neighbouring houses?"

"Not really. No one seems to have noticed anyone matching the woman's description hanging around the area."

"Hmm… okay, it's back to square one for us then. Galling that the son actually spoke to her and she got away."

"Incredibly. I'll send a few patrols out to the area today, just in case someone else comes forward who wasn't around last night."

"Thanks. I appreciate it." Sam ended the call and sat there, deep in thought for a few moments. Then she took a punt and rang Zoe at work. It took a few rings before she answered.

"Hello," Zoe whispered.

"Zoe, it's DI Sam Cobbs here. Sorry, have I caught you at a bad time?"

"I'm serving in the shop. Can you make it quick?"

"Of course I can. I was wondering if your mother knew a Jim or Annie Baldwin."

A pause followed. "Their names don't mean anything. Should they?"

"Unfortunately, there has been another murder, and certain aspects of the case are similar to your mother's death, so we're linking the two cases. What we need to establish is whether or not there's a connection between the victims that will lead us back to the perpetrator."

"That's shocking. No, sorry, I don't know them at all. That's not to say that Mum didn't know them. Maybe they filled up at the petrol station."

"Possibly, we'll look into it. Before you go, what about Carl Baldwin, does that name ring a bell at all?"

Another pause pinched the line. "No, I can't say it does. I'm sorry, Inspector, I have to go, my boss is on the warpath."

"Don't worry. I'll be in touch soon." Sam ended the call and again sat there, considering what to do next. Struggling with a solution, she decided to tackle her post and leave her emails until later. She stuck with the laborious chore for thirty minutes and then returned to the incident room. "Anything to report?"

Claire was the first to raise her hand. "I may have something, boss."

Sam wandered over and peered at Claire's screen. "What's that?"

"I did some digging into the financial side of things and spotted something very strange, once again."

"Which is?"

She circled the screen with her finger. "A few months ago, Jim Baldwin withdrew forty thousand from an ISA he had with his bank and deposited it with this company, Hall's Investments."

"Have you run their details through the system?"

"I have and I've come up blank for a second time. Well, sort of. As soon as that money was sent to the firm, it looks like it closed down."

"Jesus, so are we saying that someone is starting up these fake businesses, hooking investors with the intention of robbing them of their savings?"

Claire shrugged. "That seems a likely scenario to me."

"We need to find out who and why."

Claire sighed. "Where do I start with that?"

"Get on to the fraud squad, get their advice. Run the names of the two companies past them, see if they've had any dealings with them, and we'll go from there. Good work, Claire."

"Not sure I deserve the praise just yet."

Sam smiled and patted her on the shoulder. She moved around the room to Liam. "Any further news on the vehicle?"

"I managed to track it down on the CCTV footage close to the estate where the second murder happened and made a comparison to the one sitting outside the garage. In my opinion they're the same vehicle. Here's the thing." He pulled up an image on the screen and pointed at it. "In this vehicle there are two people, and in the one used at the second scene there's only the driver."

"The plot thickens. Did you get a close-up on the number plate? Are you sure they're the same vehicle?"

Liam's mouth twisted. "I wouldn't be willing to place my wages on it just yet, but it does seem a huge coincidence."

"The trouble is, I don't believe in them. We need cold hard facts."

"I know and I feel gutted that I can't supply any as yet. Give me time."

"That's a commodity we don't have much of, Liam. The sooner we catch this bitch the better. What if she has a whole list of people she's determined to knock off?"

"I know. I'll stick with it, unless you want me to move on to something else?"

"I don't. It's vital we come up with something we can use, pertaining to the vehicle. At the moment, it seems to be a valuable link between both cases."

Liam nodded, and she moved around the room, ending up at her partner's desk.

"Anything new here, Bob?"

"I've been trawling through the database, searching for the woman. No good so far. Her teeth are making me wonder if she's had treatment lately. Might be worth ringing round a few of the dentists in the area to find out."

"I bet they've been inundated with people wanting that type of treatment in the last few years, but it might be worth a try. Something is better than nothing, eh?"

"I'll get on it now. But then, there's a possibility the killer isn't from around this area."

"If you want to put obstructions in the way. Let's get past that, partner, and work with what we have at our disposal."

"On it now."

Sam drifted back to the whiteboard and jotted down the links they had obtained so far between the two crimes. The car was the biggest link, well, that and the vast amount of funds that had been transferred from each of the victims' accounts. The only drawback that she could tell with that was that the transfers had taken place months ago, so why had the killer returned now to finish off the victims? Why didn't they do it at the time the transfers were made?

"Boss, I've got something on the car," Liam called over to gain her attention.

Sam was at his desk like an Exocet missile. "What?"

"On the CCTV footage from a camera just on the outskirts of the town. I followed it from camera to camera until I found this." He zoomed in on the number plate.

"The full plate. This is fantastic news, except we already know the plate was stolen off a Ford Ka. Sorry, maybe I should have passed that snippet of information on before now. Nice try, Liam. What we need to do is search for the vehicle on the night of Tammy's murder, see if this woman used the same number plate or if the car had the original one."

"Too bad. Okay, there again, the killer might have a penchant for toying with the police and picked up the trick of nicking number plates to cover their tracks."

"Seems the more likely scenario, doesn't it?"

"I'm going to keep the pressure up on the lab, see if they've got anywhere with Tammy's phone yet."

"What about the second victim, was his phone found at the scene?" Bob asked.

"I'm not sure, I need to check with Des."

"We don't need the phones, not really," Claire piped up.

Sam stopped and thought over her suggestion. "You're right, all we need are the victims' phone numbers. Another job for you to do for me, Claire. Here are Carl's details. Can you contact him and get his father's number?"

"I'll do it now, boss. By the way, I forgot to mention that Tammy's boss rang. He contacted all his staff, and nothing. Which brings me back to the ATMs. I should have told you yesterday, they all drew a blank, too. The person drawing out the money from Tammy's account wore a disguise at the machine and covered their face with a hoodie."

"Bugger, not so good. Okay, thanks for tying up the loose ends, Claire. I'll get on to the lab." She walked into her office. It was always good to keep on top of them throughout a case.

The news was disappointing. The lab hadn't even started the analysis of the phone yet as they had been inundated with other work. Sam let her feelings be known and hung up. Her job was harder than people appreciated at times. Keeping all the balls up in the air was never an easy task. Thank goodness she had people like Claire on her team who invariably pulled out an ace card now and again.

CHAPTER 7

*S*he had been watching from a distance for a while now, having arrived at the location at the same time as the woman's relatives had, en masse, which had pissed her off. She was in two minds whether to drive off and return another day, but killers had to go by instinct, and tonight, she had the feeling that this would be the right time to end the woman's life. Her insides twisted into a bigger knot the more she waited, though. She'd already wasted two hours of her evening. How much longer was she supposed to wait, or be prepared to wait?

Turning the key in the ignition, she growled, disappointed that she would need to leave, but more importantly, that her killer instinct or enthusiasm would need to be parked to one side for the evening. It wasn't her fault that the woman's dumb family had showed up. She should have been relieved that she wasn't already inside the woman's house when the family arrived. That would have been another close shave she could do without.

A grin emerged as she reflected on her previous

encounter. He was a dish, the victim's son. Had she met him elsewhere, she would have been tempted to take things further with him. As it was, her need to get away from the crime scene far outweighed her need to get laid.

Her interest piqued. The front door had opened, and two children left the house and were playing chase in the front garden and out onto the pavement. The younger female was next, followed by the male. He stopped to give the old lady a kiss on both cheeks. She was beaming, happy to see her family.

Pretending to be studying a map, Jennifer kept one eye on the family. The woman waved her relatives off and then went back into the house.

Jennifer waited until the family left the area and there was no one else hanging around to see her enter the house. She knew this evening's job would be a swift one. She had a time restraint hanging around her neck tonight; she had to meet up with Phil later to discuss other hits they had lined up. With the coast now all clear, she left the driver's seat and removed her trusty bag from the boot then trotted across the road to the house. With a disarming smile in place, she rang the bell and waited patiently.

The woman took her time opening the door. "Oh, I know you, don't I?"

"That's right. I have a few queries about the last transaction you made with us and thought I'd drop by in person to run through them with you."

"Ah, that sounds like a good idea. I get far too flustered discussing my finances over the phone. Come in, sorry, I've forgotten your name?"

"It's Jennifer, Mrs Davidson."

"Call me Karen, Mrs Davidson sounds too formal even to my ears. Would you like a drink? I've just this second made a pot of tea. My family visited earlier and drained me. I was trying to recover over a nice calming drink."

"Boisterous grandchildren for you to contend with, I daresay."

"How did you guess? My theory is that my son and his wife give the children far too many sweets and it makes them hyper. I'm getting too old to tolerate that kind of malarkey these days. Come in out of the cold. There's a real chill in the air this week, isn't there? Far colder than the weatherman said it was going to be. Mind you, when are they ever right?"

Jennifer smiled and entered the house when Karen stepped back into the hallway. "So true. Don't bother about making me a drink, hopefully I won't be here too long."

"No problem, let me know if you change your mind."

"I will."

Karen led the way into her dated lounge. The sofa was covered in a floral print that reminded Jennifer of her grandmother's. Anger built. She'd hated her grandmother. To the outside world she used to display angelic tendencies, but once the door was shut she turned nasty. Whipping Jennifer, locking her in a cupboard for her entire stay. She even threatened to kill her mother, her own daughter, if Jennifer ever uttered a word about what happened when she'd frequently stayed with her grandmother. Her childhood had been spent mostly in fear, meaning she had been reserved at school, which in turn had led her to being a prime candidate for the bullies to descend upon.

"Are you all right, dear? You seemed very distant there for a moment or two, as if you had something on your mind."

"Sorry, it's been a problematic day, and I learnt on the way over here that there had been a death in the family."

"Really? You have my condolences. Was it anyone close?"

"Kind of. My grandmother. She was in her nineties, she had a good innings." *How the lies tumble out of my mouth so easily when pushed. The old crow died years ago, when I was in my teens.*

"Please, take a seat. Ah, so it was expected then. It doesn't make it any easier to deal with, though, does it?"

"No, it was heartbreaking to hear the news. I only visited her at the weekend, she seemed pretty good then. Mum said the decline in her has been a gradual one over the week. I've been too busy to go and see her this week. Phil has me working all hours at the moment, you know how strict some bosses can be."

"I do. I had a tyrant of a boss, many years ago. Was a stickler about me working to the correct times of my shifts, except when it suited him. One night he begged me to stay behind and type up some urgent reports for a last-minute meeting he'd scheduled for the next day. I told him I couldn't as my husband had bought tickets for a show that I was desperate to see. He ended up on his knees, pleading with me and even said he would pay me treble time. Geoff, my hubby, was livid when I rang him and explained the situation. He slammed the phone down on me, but what else could I do? I had already agreed to work the extra hours, and my boss would have made my life hell if I'd gone back on my word. Anyway, to cut a long story short, I was getting something out of the filing cabinet when the boss's door opened. I didn't think anything of it, thought he was getting himself a coffee from the table behind me, that was until I felt his hand on my backside. I spun around, and he pinned me to the cabinet and took advantage of me. I won't go into further detail... needless to say, I was distraught, too traumatised to complete the task I had been paid to do. I ended up grabbing my handbag and tore out of the office."

"No. What happened the next day, when you went back to work?"

"I didn't. I called in sick. Which wasn't a lie, I was sick to my stomach every time I thought about his hands running over my body, him plastering my face with slobbery wet kisses." She placed a hand to her mouth. "God, I'm heaving now just reliving the story. Not sure why I did that, I've never revealed that to anyone before. Please forgive me."

Jennifer smiled. "Nothing to forgive. I'm sorry you had to deal with such crap from your boss. From what I hear from my friends, most bosses seem to think you owe them something, don't they?"

"Well, this one did. His wife had recently kicked him out, and he thought he'd take advantage of the situation of having me all to himself that evening. He was vile."

"Did you ever work for him again?"

"Only for a week or so. Fortunately, a friend of mine told me that her firm were recruiting extra secretaries and that she would put my name forward if I was interested. I rang her the next day, and the rest is history."

"How did your boss take your resignation?"

She rolled her eyes and took a sip from her cup of tea. "Not well at all. Begged me to stay, on his knees again, he was. I remained strong and told him I would never work another day for him and that he was lucky I didn't tell my husband, or worse still, go to the police. He promised me he would never do the same again."

"His type will never change. Once a groper, always a groper, eh?"

"I agree. Now, then, I've taken up far too much of your time this evening, what is it you have come to see me about?"

Jennifer hesitated. She liked this old woman, and she wondered if she had the courage to go through with her mission, that was until Karen's face morphed into her grandmother's old, wizened features and her grandmother's voice chirped in her head.

You're a hopeless waste of space, always have been, since the day you were born. Should have died at birth. They used oxygen to keep you alive, that was a waste as well. In an incubator for weeks, you were, other babies died all around you. I used to visit you and wish you were dead. Feeble baby, not worth the hassle your parents had to deal with. Had you been a dog you would have been put down. Vile child. You had no right pulling through that experience. You should have gone back to Hell, where you belonged.

"You've gone again, dear. Are you sure you should be here this evening? You're clearly suffering from grief, whether you care to admit it or not. You should go home, stop punishing yourself and give in to the grief."

Jennifer stared at Karen, still seeing her grandmother's evil features before her. Her hand dipped into the bag, and she clutched the knife, wincing as the blade nicked her finger.

"Are you okay, Jennifer. You've gone very pale. Here, let me get you a drink. I won't take no for an answer this time. Tea or coffee?"

"A coffee would be lovely. Thank you, I'll be all right in a second or two."

Karen leaned forward and patted the back of her hand. "It's the shock. It's going to take a while to get over it. You were obviously very close to your grandmother."

If only you knew the truth.

Karen left the room, and Jennifer tipped her head back against the sofa and closed her eyes. Then she did the unthinkable and fell asleep. She woke up with Karen gently shaking her a few minutes later.

"I'm so sorry, I don't know what came over me."

"That's all right. Like I said, it'll be the shock. Umm... were you aware that your hand is bleeding?"

Jennifer stared at the dried patch of blood on her hand.

"Oh my, I wasn't. Would it be okay if I use your sink in the kitchen?"

"No, use the downstairs cloakroom instead. First door on the right in the hallway."

Feeling overwhelmed and suffocated by Karen's close proximity, she left the room to regain her composure. Her reflection caught her attention in the mirror above the basin.

You're visibly falling apart girl. Get a grip of yourself and finish the job off.

She ran the water until it got warm and then washed the blood from her hand. After drying her hands on a towel, she left the room and returned to the lounge.

"Are you feeling better now, dear? How did you cut yourself?"

Jennifer nodded and picked up her bag. "On this." She removed the knife and held it to the shocked Karen's throat. "Scream and I'll end your life right now."

"I... won't... I... promise. What do you want from me?"

"Every piece of paperwork pertaining to the investments you made with us."

"May I ask why? What's wrong with them? Has something happened to my money? Where is it? None of this is making..."

"Shut up! Wind your fucking neck in, for fuck's sake."

Karen pulled her head back and in doing so nicked her throat on the blade. "Ouch, that hurt. I'm sorry. I'm scared. I tend to witter on when I'm scared. Please, you don't have to hurt me. I'll give you what you want, no more questions asked, I promise."

"Where are they?"

"I keep them upstairs, under my bed, shall I get them for you?"

"I'll come with you. No tricks, old lady, or I'll kill you."

"Goodness me, I won't cause you any problems. Please, I don't want to die. I have so much to live for. I know I complain about them all the time but I want to see my grandchildren grow up, they're showing so much promise. I want to see what they get up to in later life. I won't be able to do that from my grave."

Jennifer leaned in close, her forehead resting against Karen's. "I told you to shut up."

"I will. I'm sorry."

Jennifer tugged on her arm to get Karen to her feet. She led the way up the stairs to the main bedroom. It felt cold in the room, not surprising as it had bare floorboards and only a small rug close to the bed.

"I'll have to move the bed. I have a secret compartment underneath, in one of the floorboards. You'll have to help me, it's a heavy wooden frame. My son treated me to it from Oak Furniture Land."

"I don't give a shit where he bought it, just move it. Where's the hiding place?"

"At the top. We'll need to shift the whole bed either to the side or pull it down a little. I don't want to scratch my wooden floor, though, so please be careful because Lee only sanded them a few years ago for me."

Jennifer puffed out her cheeks and shook her head. "Enough, I don't want the ins and outs of your sad life, just shut up!"

"I'm sorry. I always speak a lot when I'm nervous. Please forgive me."

"To the side, are you ready?" Jennifer said, after hearing enough of the woman's chuntering to last her a lifetime.

"I should put a blanket down to save the floor," Karen insisted.

"Just do it." Jennifer held the knife to Karen's throat again, her intentions clear.

"All right. On your head be it. Don't be surprised if Lee comes knocking on your door for compensation."

Jennifer's eyes widened as the anger pulsed through her veins. "Last warning. Now shift the damn bed with me." Jennifer pushed with her free hand, but the frame was so heavy she was forced to put the knife down on the bed and shove it with both hands. Karen was as much use as a fart in a colander. The old woman was left breathing heavily after her exertions.

"I need water. Please, get me a glass of water, I need to take one of my heart tablets or I'll end up in hospital."

"Jesus wept. I'm in charge here, not you. Where's the relevant floorboard?"

Karen pointed at one of the floorboards that had been cut in half. "That one there. My tablets…" Karen demanded weakly before she collapsed onto the bed.

"Where are they?"

"In the en suite, the cabinet above the sink. The blue ones. Hurry… please."

Jennifer debated whether to get the tablets or just to kill the woman there and then. In the end, reluctantly, she ran into the bathroom and returned with the pot of pills. "Are these them… where are you?" The room was empty. Straining an ear, she couldn't hear any movement on the stairs which meant the woman was probably hiding somewhere up here. "Oh, Karen, where are you? Come out, come out, wherever you are."

Silence. Anger piquing once more, Jennifer ran to the bank of built-in wardrobes along the far wall and tore every door open. She lunged with the knife, jabbing at the dresses in case the woman was hiding at the back. She wasn't in there. If she was, Jennifer hadn't found her. Her patience was wearing thin now. She needed that paperwork, and quickly.

She was on her way back towards the floorboards when

something whacked her across the back of the neck. She collapsed onto the bed, her head swimming, Karen standing over her, sneering at her.

"Thought you'd get the better of me, did you?" Karen had the knife in her hand, waving it back and forth.

"What the fuck are you doing, Karen?"

"You think every old woman is incapable of defending herself. I'm ready to put that myth to bed. You're despicable, coming here like this. Tell me why you're here, the truth this time."

"I told you the truth, I need the paperwork."

"Why?"

"I need to bury it," Jennifer replied, her thinking more responsive than before.

"Bury it? Why?"

Jennifer looked over Karen's shoulder and gasped. Karen fell for the well-oiled trick, and Jennifer karate-chopped Karen's arm. Instantly, the knife fell to the floor, and Jennifer was the quickest to retrieve it.

The older woman's face dropped. "Thought you could get the better of me, did you? Where's the paperwork? Now! Stop treating me like an idiot or I'll kill you and then go after your son and his family."

"I'll get it for you."

Jennifer placed the knife to Karen's throat, issuing an unspoken warning of what would happen if Karen slipped up again. She flipped one end of the floorboard, and it immediately revealed a plastic bag which Karen removed and planted on top of the bed.

"It's all in there. Safe and out of harm's way, or it used to be until you came along."

Jennifer stared at the bag. "Open it. Empty the contents out."

"Why? It's all there."

"Do it!"

Karen took a step closer to the bed and tipped the carrier bag up. The contents scattered across the pink floral duvet, and Jennifer stared at the array of forms before her. One in particular stood out, the woman's Will.

"This is what I'm after."

"Why?"

Jennifer winked at Karen and tapped the side of her nose. "None of your business."

"What now?"

"Now, I tie you up and leave you here to rot. At least that's what I should do, after your foiled heroic antics."

"No doubt you would have done the same if you had found yourself in my situation."

Jennifer grinned. "Probably," she admitted. "Get on the bed and prop the pillows behind you."

"And if I don't?"

Jennifer raised an eyebrow. "You really want to challenge me? Don't you want to see your family again?"

"Yes, I'm sorry. I'll do it now. Don't hurt me."

"Shut that mouth of yours for a change and hop up on the bed."

Karen sat on the edge and swung her legs up. She settled against the pillows and stared at Jennifer. "Now what?"

"This," Jennifer said in a matter-of-fact tone and took a step forward.

Her right hand extended, one fatal slice across the throat, and it was all over. The blood erupted from the wound and covered the quilt and Karen's lap within seconds. Karen's eyes had widened, and her hands instantly clutched at her throat, a gurgling noise emerging from the wound. A few seconds later, all was quiet as Karen's head lolled to the right.

Jennifer deposited the will in her bag, along with another couple of papers she felt might come in handy later. She paused in the hallway and took the time to wipe away the blood spattered across her cheek, then left the house. With her composure gathered once more, she made her way out to the car. With no great urgency to get away and not wanting to draw attention to herself, she calmly slipped behind the steering wheel.

CHAPTER 8

Sam was completing her morning chore of going through the post the following day when the call came in from Nick, the desk sergeant.

"Sorry to trouble you so early, ma'am. I've been notified of a nine-nine-nine emergency call coming in and I think it's something that might be of interest to you."

Sam put down her pen and frowned. "You've got my attention. What is it?"

"A woman has been murdered in her own home. She was found by her daughter this morning. Her throat has been cut, and her personal paperwork was lying on the bed beside her."

"Shit! Give me the address, I'll get over there now."

"It's number six Wainwright's Close at Camerton."

"I know it. Thanks, Nick."

Sam hung up and slipped her jacket off the back of the chair. She picked up her mobile and headed for the door. "We've got yet another murder. A woman with her throat cut, found by her daughter out at Camerton. As soon as we have any further details, we'll let you know, Claire."

"I'll be waiting for your call, boss. Do you have a name I can be getting on with?"

"I haven't, sorry. We'll be in touch soon. Come on, Bob, time's a wasting."

Bob jumped out of his seat and thrust his arms into his jacket.

DES and his team were already at the scene. Sam and Bob togged up in their protective suits and shoes, signed the log and entered the house.

"Des, it's Sam, are you upstairs?"

"Yes, come on up, but only if you've got the necessary protective gear on."

"We have, don't worry." Sam climbed the stairs, taking in her surroundings on the way. It was obvious the victim cared a lot about her family, given that there were a lot of photos adorning the hallway walls on the way up the stairs. "Such a shame. Why?" she asked quietly, more to herself than to her partner.

"Sorry, did you speak?"

"Not really. Just assessing what's going on around us."

Sam reached the top of the stairs and continued along the landing, dipping her head into every room until she found the one she was looking for. "Ah, here you are. This place is huge. Nice house."

"Are you here to admire the design of the building or to solve a crime?"

"The latter, Mr Grumpy. It was merely an observation, there's no need for you to snap my head off. Take a chill pill every now and again."

Des stared at her and narrowed his eyes. "I'll ignore that particular jibe as it's still fairly early in the day."

"In other words, you can't come up with a suitable retort."

"Oh, I can, the question is, do I want to? The answer to that one is categorically no, I'm far too busy here."

Sam's attention shifted to the blood-soaked victim lying on top of the bed. "Shit. That's bad. I'm surmising that a lot of anger went into this attack?"

"Your assumption would be correct. As far as I can tell it was one slice across the throat that did the damage."

Sam glanced around the room.

"The bed has been moved," Bob said as if reading her mind.

"I'm assuming her paperwork was stored underneath." Sam got down on her knees to have a closer look. "A floorboard has been modified, probably to provide a hiding place."

"The lengths some people will go to," Bob muttered.

Sam got to her feet, her suit rustling noisily. "A lot of good it did her in the end. I'm calling it, the three murders are linked."

Des's gloved hands met in a slow, deliberate clap. "She's good. Umm... which is why I requested your attendance at the scene."

Sam grinned. "Sorry, don't knock the stuffing out of me, it shows I'm on the ball. Anyway, I was thinking out loud."

"If you say so," Des grumbled.

"Do you have an inkling what's missing?" Sam pointed at the paperwork.

"A quick assessment leads me to think the most important items are missing. For instance, birth and marriage certs, passport, and even a copy of the Will, if she had one in place."

"Sounds logical to me. I was told the daughter found her. Where is she?"

"The neighbour came out on that side." He jabbed his thumb to the right. "Invited her and her brother into the house. They seemed out of sorts, as one would imagine, but went willingly. Better than sitting in their cars on a cold and wet day like today."

"Fair enough. We'll nip next door and see them. Any other evidence?" Sam pointed at a numbered marker in the centre of the room, highlighting a small patch of blood.

"Possibly. We've marked it for a reason," Des replied, his sarcasm evident in his tone.

"Pardon me for having an inquisitive notion."

Des grinned. "You're pardoned. Now, I need you two to get out of my hair and let me and the team get on with our work."

"We're out of here. You don't need to tell us twice."

"Makes a change. No doubt I'll see you later."

"You might do."

THEY STRIPPED off their protective suits and deposited them in the black bag then rang the bell next door. A worried-looking woman in her sixties opened the door.

Sam produced her ID. "I'm DI Sam Cobbs, and this is my partner, DS Bob Jones."

"We've been expecting you. I'm Carolyn Smith. Karen was one of my dearest friends. I'm mortified that she has been taken from us like this. Her children, Lee and Mandy, are in there, absolutely beside themselves."

"I'm sure. It must have been an horrendous experience for the daughter to have found her mother like that. Do you think they are up for a chat with us?"

"I'm sure. They'll want the investigation underway at the earliest opportunity, I would imagine."

"Of course, we'll ensure that happens, once we've interviewed them."

"Very well, they're through here, in the lounge."

Sam and Bob wiped their feet on the mat outside in the porch and entered the house.

"Do you want us to take our shoes off?" Sam asked.

"No, they'll be clean enough. I'm not that particular, that's why I specifically chose a darker shade of carpet."

"Makes sense to me," Sam replied with a slight smile.

Carolyn led them into a brightly lit lounge that had a mulberry colour feature wall and a log burner that was emitting a welcome and inviting heat. Sitting on the couch, their arms wrapped around each other, were two people who Sam presumed were the victim's son and daughter.

"This is DI Cobbs and DS Jones. Mandy and Lee, Karen's children. Right, I'm going to leave you to speak in private. Can I get anyone a drink?"

Sam and Bob both shook their heads.

"Can I get another coffee please, Carolyn?" Lee asked.

"Coming right up. What about you, Mand?"

"I'm all right, but thanks for asking."

Carolyn left the room. Sam and Bob made themselves comfortable on the sofa opposite to where Lee and Mandy were sitting. Sam was grateful they were further away from the roaring fire, sensing that she would be stripping off her excess clothes soon enough, judging by the amount of heat the fire was throwing out.

"It's warm in here," Sam said.

"Is it? I'm freezing," Mandy said, her voice trembling with either the cold or the emotion, or maybe a mixture of both.

Lee took his sister's hands in his own and vigorously rubbed them. "It's the shock, sweetheart. Try to put the image out of your mind. You're going to have to, otherwise you'll never be able to move on with your life."

"It's too soon to even contemplate doing that, Lee. You didn't see her, lying there... covered in her own blood. It was like something out of a horror movie, not that I've ever seen one before. They've always been too gory for me. To be confronted with an image like that... involving your own sweet mother... it's just... I don't know, words are failing me at this sad time. I'm so angry that someone believed they had a right to go into Mum's home and take her life. What purpose did it serve? She wasn't robbed of anything of value, I checked all her jewellery, it was all there, the same with the TV and everything else they could flog for money. None of this is making any bloody sense to me at all."

"Nor me. Let's try and remain calm and see what the police officers have to say about all of this, because it's beyond me. I'm struggling to come to terms with what appears to be a nonsensical killing, carried out by a mindless jerk."

Sam sighed. "I have to start off by saying how sorry we are for your loss. I also need to tell you that this is not the first crime of this nature that has come to our attention this week."

"Come to your attention? What does that even mean?" Lee queried.

"We're investigating three very similar crimes this week which have all taken place in this area. What we're having trouble with is the why. Can you shed any light on that side of things for us?"

"No, definitely not. Are you insinuating our mother invited this person into her house and allowed them to kill her?"

"No. Far from it. What I'm trying to establish is if your mother had mentioned having any worries or problems in her life recently."

"What? That could have led to her death? That is what you're asking, isn't it? Why don't you come right out and say it? You think she brought her murder on herself, don't you?"

Sam shook her head, her heart beating faster by the

second. "I'm sorry, I really didn't mean it to come across like that."

"Our mother was recovering from breast cancer. That's why I was here today, to pick her up for an appointment with her consultant. He was going to give her a thorough examination and possibly give her the all-clear... there's no need for that to happen now, is there? I can't believe this has happened. We only lost Dad a few years ago, and now... Mum has gone, too. What the hell is this world coming to? Why aren't the police doing their job of protecting people?" Mandy replied.

"We're doing our best. Sometimes it's just not good enough. Did your mother live here alone?"

"Yes. We know it's a large house. Mum was in the process of listing the property with a couple of agents. It's taken her a while to come round to the idea. She used to feel Dad all around her and said he would be angry if she sold the house too soon. The cost-of-living crisis finally hit home. We've been telling her for years that the property takes far too much to run to warrant one person living there alone. It took months of badgering her for her to finally concede that we were right. I was going to help her clear out some of the kitchen cupboards today, after we came back from the hospital... It wasn't to be."

"She'd made appointments with the agents?" Sam asked.

"That's right. Just to get a valuation and to have a chat about what fees they were going to charge if a sale went through. She was resigned to moving on, had come to terms with letting go of the past... of all the happy memories the family had made growing up in that house."

"Can I ask how your father died?"

"He had a brain tumour. His passing came not long after his diagnosis, which was a relief as he went downhill rapidly," Lee replied. "That was three years ago in June. Mum had not long come to terms with his death when she was diagnosed with breast cancer. At first, she refused to have treatment, told us she wanted to join Dad, but then..." He gripped his sister's hand and kissed the back of it. "Mandy worked her magic to persuade Mum it was in all our interests not to give in to the disease. We loved our parents more than anything else in this world, Inspector."

"I'm sure you did. Has your mother mentioned meeting anyone new in the last few weeks or months?"

"You think someone she knew would have coldheartedly taken her life?"

"I'm not sure. We need to carry out the necessary digging to see what comes to our attention. As things stand, we have very little to go on to begin our investigation."

"What about the other cases you mentioned? Are there any similarities in the crimes? If there are, won't that give you a lead to start with?"

"The only thing that is standing out to me at present is the fact that your mother's personal papers were visible in the room."

"They were?" Mandy asked.

She must have been too shocked to have noticed them. "Yes, they were spread out on the bed, however, the pathologist believes that certain important documents were missing."

"Missing? Such as?" Lee demanded.

"A few certificates, birth and marriage, possibly your father's death certificate as well. There were no passports found, and maybe a Will, if your mother had got around to making one."

The siblings stared at one another, then they shrugged.

Lee faced Sam and said quietly, "There was definitely a Will. Up until last year, Mum didn't have one in place. We hounded her until she finally buckled under the pressure.

Actually, it was Mandy's husband, Ray, who said it would be a good idea to get everything tied up early."

"Ray? Is he around?"

"No, he works away from home during the week, down in London. He's overseeing a huge building project down there, a water plant. He's good with money. Can talk the hind leg off a donkey about investments. Not such a great topic at the moment, given the state the economy is in. We have Liz Truss to thank for that."

"I agree. The country is going to be in an absolute mess for years to come, thanks to that shower doing their best to destabilise our economy. Do you have a family solicitor you use?"

Lee frowned. "Yes, Simons and Bartlett in Workington. Why?"

"They'll probably have a copy of your mother's Will."

"That's a good idea. Should I ring them? Is there any need at this stage?"

Sam smiled. "We'll chase it up. It would be remiss of us not to look into it further. Is it just the two of you, or do you have other siblings?"

"No, it's just Mandy and I. Mum and Dad did have another baby in between us, but he died after a few days. Heart complications. The doctors felt it was better to let the little one go."

"How sad. Sorry to hear that."

Lee smiled at his sister. "We still visit the grave, don't we, love? Despite not knowing the little one."

"He was a part of us, whether he survived or not."

"What about other family members, anyone we should know about?"

"Not really. The odd distant cousin dotted here and there around the UK."

Sam smiled. "The usual then. I have to ask if either you or

your mother know these people: Tammy Callard or Jim Baldwin."

The siblings held each other's gaze for a few seconds until they both shook their heads.

"No, should we?" Lee asked.

"They're the other victims who have sadly lost their lives, the crimes we're also investigating."

"Ah, right. Let me try and think harder, in that case." He paused, and then his nose wrinkled and mouth drooped with disappointment. "Sorry, no, can't say I recognise the names at all. Mandy?"

"No, I don't either. I wish I did, it would help you catch the killer quicker, wouldn't it?"

"It would. Don't worry. I don't want you putting yourselves under any further unnecessary stress today."

"Is there anything else we can help you with?"

"I don't suppose your mother had any kind of security cameras throughout the house or grounds, did she?"

"Not that I'm aware of. We discussed the possibility of getting some fitted around five years ago. I recall my father being keener than my mother on the idea at the time, but nothing came of it."

"Not to worry."

Carolyn entered the room with two mugs. She gave one to Lee and then took a seat at the small table situated in the bay window. "Don't mind me, I have a few letters I need to reply to."

"It's okay. I think we've just about finished here anyway, unless either of you would like to ask us anything before we leave?" Sam replied.

"Are we safe?" Mandy asked.

"We have no reason to believe the killer will return, they haven't revisited either of the other families. What I will add is that it's better to remain vigilant at all times, just in case."

Sam rose from her seat, and Bob tucked his notebook into his pocket and did the same.

"I'll show you to the door," Lee said.

In the hallway, he peered over his shoulder at the room they had just left and whispered, "Are you sure the killer won't come after us? What if you're wrong?"

"All I can do is reassure you, although I can't offer any kind of guarantee, it would be wrong of me to do such a thing."

"I can understand. Maybe we should keep our families together for a few days, to ensure their safety, just until you've caught the killer."

"Might be a good idea. Take care. Here's one of my cards. Any problems, ring me day or night."

"Thank you, we'll only call if it's an extreme emergency."

Sam smiled and shook his hand. "Again, I'm sorry for your loss."

"Please, you have to help us find who did this. I can't think of a single reason why Mum should die this way, it doesn't make sense to me in the slightest."

"Don't worry, we're going to do all we can to find the person responsible. My team has an excellent record."

"Good to hear. Thank you, Inspector. Will you stay in touch with us as the investigation progresses?"

"I will, if you want me to. Why don't you give me a call every couple of days, for an update?"

"I'll do that." He opened the front door, they stepped out of the house, and he closed it behind them.

"Another nice family's life ruined," Bob said when they were halfway up the path.

"It never gets any easier, talking to the relatives. All the more reason for us to get on with the case, though. Let's get back to the station, see what the others have managed to dig up for us."

. . .

AFTER A SOLEMN DRIVE BACK, Sam and Bob entered the incident room to find the others with their heads down getting on with their work. A sense of pride filled Sam. Not every inspector oversaw such a dedicated team.

"How are things going, guys? Any updates for us?"

Alex cleared his throat. "I had a peep at the victim's bank account, went back a couple of years, and yes, you've guessed it, a vast sum of money was transferred at the end of last year."

Sam removed her jacket, hooked it over her arm and perched on the desk behind her. "Vast sum? How much are we talking about, Alex?"

"A lot more than the previous two victims," he replied.

Sam gestured for him to hurry up.

"Hold on to your hat, boss, I'm coming to it. Five hundred grand."

Sam propelled herself off the desk and approached him. "Did I hear correctly? Half a million?"

"You did. She must have been a very wealthy woman to consider tying up that amount."

Sam glanced over at Bob. "Would you have thought that, given the house and area we've just come from? Not that it was a shitty area... yeah, I'm going to end my sentence right there before I get myself into bother."

Bob sniggered. "I should."

"What I'm trying to say, without offending anyone or the area she lives in, in case any of you have relatives around there, she hid her wealth well. Yes, she had a nice house, but there was nothing grand about it from what we could tell. Okay, I'm getting off track here. Where did the money go? Please tell me you've had a chance to trace it?"

Alex tapped the side of his nose and smiled. "It was paid

to Romney Finances. And yes, you've guessed it, the company no longer exists."

"What the actual fuck? Three different companies, and they've all gone bust. Right, we need to do some more digging into these companies, this is really starting to tick me off now."

Alex raised a finger. "I haven't had long to check but I did a Google search and found a few old Twitter threads for each of the companies."

Sam inclined her head. "And?"

"And, they turned out to be complaints, every single one of them. All of them warning people not to deal with the respective companies. I suppose by then, the people putting the tweets out there had already suffered their losses."

"Is there a way of tracing these people? Sorry, I'm not all that familiar with Twitter. Don't people tend to make up all sorts of weird and wonderful personas on that social network site?"

"You're right. Most of the time, that's ultimately what happens, but I can give it a go. I could also put out a call on Twitter, name the companies involved and see if anyone responds to the Tweets, you know, warning me off, and go from there."

"Sounds like an excellent plan to me, Alex. While you're on there, can you also do a search for other financial businesses that might have gone belly up?"

He frowned and hitched up his right shoulder. "I can try. It's going to be difficult finding results without mentioning the company names in the Tweets."

Sam winked and patted him on the shoulder. "If anyone can do it, you can. I have complete and utter faith in you."

Suzanna raised her hand to speak. "I might have a suggestion there, boss."

"Which is?"

"Alex could put out a Tweet for a recommendation for an investment company. In my minimal experience on the site, people are quick to tell you who to avoid."

"There you go, Alex. Thinking about it, why don't you and Suzanna team up on this one? You both have personal Twitter accounts you can use for the purpose, it would be better if you steered clear of using the police one which is at our disposal."

Alex shifted his chair over to Suzanna's desk, and they shared a joke then pulled a serious face and put their heads together. Sam's ears pricked up; the phone in her office was ringing. She trotted across the incident room to answer the call.

"DI Sam Cobbs, how can I help?"

"It's only me, ma'am. Nick on reception."

"Hi, Nick, what's up?"

"I've had some interesting feedback from my officers doing the house-to-house enquiries at the latest murder scene."

"I'm listening." Sam sat at her desk and picked up a pen.

"A couple of the neighbours noticed a silver SUV sitting in the road outside the victim's house. One of them also said they saw a woman with long hair get in the vehicle and drive off."

"Hmm… did they say what time?"

"Sometime after seven, they struggled to nail it down better than that."

"It doesn't matter, it's good enough for me. We'll see if we can trace the vehicle. Pass on my gratitude to your team, Nick, they've come up trumps again."

"They'll be thrilled to hear that, ma'am."

"If anything else crops up, ring me ASAP, if you would?"

"I will, don't worry."

Sam ended the call and returned to the incident room.

"Well, if we weren't already in the process of linking the murder cases, we would be now. House-to-house enquiries have thrown up a woman with long hair getting into a silver SUV outside the victim's property at around seven. The neighbour wasn't able to narrow it down any further than that." Sam's gaze drifted around the room to Liam. "You know what I'm going to ask next, Liam."

"I'm on it, boss."

"If we can find that vehicle, maybe we're in with a shout of catching up with this woman. All right, it's obvious she's switching plates to stay ahead of us, but she has to slip up one of these days." Sam crossed the room to Claire. "How are you getting on, Claire? You've been a little quiet, although every time I've looked up, I've seen you beavering away over here."

"I'm darting down different avenues that have opened up for us, boss. Nothing concrete to report back on so far, but I sense I'm getting close."

"Have you heard back from the Fraud Squad yet? Do I need to start chasing someone up over there?"

"No, they said they would get back to me within the next twenty-four hours. I'd rather not piss anyone off over there, for now."

"If they're slack in their response, give me a nudge, and I'll have a word in the right ear over there."

"I'll do that."

Sam continued around the room to Alex and Suzanna. "And what about you guys?"

"We've put a number of Tweets out there, boss. Waiting for people to come back to us. It's all about the hashtags we've used, they'll do the trick, I'm sure," Alex replied.

Sam raised a hand. "It's all beyond me. Facebook is my limit, I can't be doing with all these WhatsApp, Twitter, TikTok et cetera, it can get far too overwhelming for a start."

Alex and Suzanna both laughed. "There are some folks out there who would call you a dinosaur, boss. Not me, of course," Alex was quick to add.

Sam shrugged and moved round the room to her partner. She threw over her shoulder, "And they'd be right. I admit it, technology and the expectations upon us to conform are beyond me. How's it going, Bob?"

"I've been trying to make sense of why the three victims have been hit financially. You have to admit, it's not something that we've seen on a regular basis."

"I agree. So?"

"As far as we're aware, the victims didn't know each other, and yet all three of them have had funds taken off them."

"Correction, the funds were transferred to dodgy accounts."

Bob placed his pen against his cheek and tapped it. "How can that happen?"

Sam's brow furrowed. "I see what you're getting at. In order to make a connection, we have to find out who the victims were in touch with in order to make the transfers."

"Exactly. Would an accountant be involved, or would the onus land on a financial advisor's shoulders?"

Sam contemplated her answer for a second or two and then plumped for the second option. "It would need to be a financial advisor. Chris had an accountant, and all he handled was the company's accounts. He refused to dish out any financial advice, such as building a pension pot or life insurance and liability insurance. Except, Chris being Chris, was always reluctant about going down that route."

"What? Are you telling me he didn't set up a pension fund, even though he was self-employed?"

Sam shook her head.

"That's ludicrous. Anything could have happened to

him... sorry, the words slipped out before I had a chance to engage my brain. He left you penniless? No insurance in place that would pay off the house if he died?" Bob said incredulously.

"Yep, no life insurance, nothing. Hey, we both know what a selfish bastard he was. Him taking his own life and straddling me with debts up to my armpits kind of proves it, doesn't it?"

"And some. I feel for you, Sam—sorry, boss—I really do."

"We're lucky in that respect. Being coppers, we pay into a pension through our salary. It takes away the uncertainty, doesn't it?"

Bob seemed down in the dumps at the revelation.

"Come on, no long faces, it is what it is. Life's too short to sit back and question the whys and wherefores of its great mysteries, like obtaining financial security for our future at our age."

"Was that Chris's argument or yours?"

Sam smiled. "Whose do you think? Anyway, enough about my dour existence, what are we going to do about our little dilemma?"

"I'm going to list the number of financial advisors there are in the area and see what I come up with."

"Good man. I'll leave you to it. Give me a shout when you find anything."

"Boss, can you spare a minute?" Liam called over. He was hunched over his keyboard, his head flicking up and down between the keyboard and the screen. "I've got a silver SUV located on the outskirts of town at seven-fifteen, which would appear to be coming from the direction of the third victim's house."

"Brilliant. Can you enhance the image of the driver on any of the cameras, Liam?"

"Not so far. All I can make out is that it's a woman."

"Keep trying. Track her route, see where she goes to."

"I will."

Sam made herself useful by pouring everyone a cup of coffee which she distributed and then dipped back into her office where she jotted down some notes of leads they needed to chase up and what the time frame was for those leads. Frustrated with keeping so many balls in the air at the same time, Sam finished her drink and returned to her partner. "Any luck?"

"I was about to come and find you. I've come across three FAs working in the Workington area and another two in Whitehaven."

"Good job. Let's stick with the local ones for now. Let's go."

"Where?" Bob asked, getting to his feet.

"To make their acquaintance."

"You're willing to risk that without obtaining any background information on the firms first?"

"You can do the necessary checks on the way. I'm going stir crazy around here and need to feel like I'm doing something important out there."

"If you say so. I'll need to jot down their addresses first."

Sam tutted. "Any decent detective worth his salt would have that information to hand by now."

"Get you! That was next on my agenda before you interrupted me."

"I apologise."

"There's a first for everything."

Sam ignored his jibe and paced the area in front of his desk until Bob slammed his pen down on his pad.

"I'm ready. You can be an impatient so-and-so at times, but I guess you're already aware of that, aren't you? Otherwise, you'd act straight-laced and professional like normal inspectors."

Sam tried to suppress the laugh tickling her throat. She managed it, too, until they reached the concrete staircase that led to the exit. "I love winding you up, it's so bloody easy at times."

He growled under his breath.

THE FIRST OFFICE was down a back street that even Sam never knew existed. "Blimey, I bet he doesn't get much passing trade, being set off the beaten track like this."

"Maybe he doesn't need it as such. Wouldn't it be a case of *needing* his services rather than wanting them?"

Sam stared at her partner, her mouth twisting from side to side. "If you say so. If I knew what you were on about."

"How you ever got to be inspector is beyond me at times. I didn't say anything that could have been construed as baffling."

Sam shared a toothy grin. "Shall we see what he has to say? I hope you've got the list of dodgy companies to hand."

"I thought you'd have them."

"I was otherwise engaged, checking on the rest of the team. The least you could have done was jotted the information down..."

Bob smiled, and Sam slyly cursed.

"You're the one winding me up now, aren't you?"

He struck a finger in the air.

They entered the office. There was a petite lady at the filing cabinet and a rotund man sitting at the desk to the rear of the room. Sam and Bob produced their warrant cards.

"DI Sam Cobbs and DS Bob Jones. Is it possible to speak to the person in charge?" Sam asked, unsure if that would be the male or female, never one to take things for granted in such situations.

"That will be Mr Hamilton. May I ask what this is about?" the woman asked.

"We're making enquiries that cover three individual cases. Is he free?" Sam's gaze drifted to the man at the rear whose ears had pricked up and who was looking their way.

"What's that, Patricia?"

"Two police officers wanting a chat with you, Mr Hamilton."

He gestured for them to join him. "Take a seat. Can Patricia get you a drink?"

"No, we're fine. We've not long had one back at the station, but thank you for the offer."

"What's this visit all about then?"

"We're dealing with some grave crimes that have taken place in the area in the past week and believe you may be able to help us."

"How so, Inspector?" He steepled his fingers under his chin.

"If I give you the names of some companies, can you tell me if you've either heard of them or had any dealings with them?"

"It's a strange request but yes, go on. I'll give it a shot."

"The first is Secured Capital."

He shook his head. "Sorry, never heard of it before."

"The second is Hall's Investments."

Again, he gave another vigorous shake of his head. "No, nothing is ringing any bells with me."

"And the final one is Romney Finances."

His eyes narrowed, and he mulled the name over for a few moments. "I don't think I've dealt with Romney Finances before. Let me check that on the system for you, just to be sure."

"That would be great, thank you. How many companies do you deal with, sir?"

"A fair amount, probably running into a hundred or more, thinking about it. I'm usually pretty good with names but I'm in my sixties now, and the memory isn't what it used to be in my younger days." He tapped at the keyboard, and his nose twitched. "No, nothing even similar to that on my system. That's not to say that these companies don't exist, it just means that I haven't had any dealings with them in the past."

"Not to worry. What about the other financial advisors in the area?"

"I'm not sure I understand your question, what about them?"

"Sorry. What I should have asked is: do you think they would know about these companies?"

He snorted. "Inspector, I'm a Financial Advisor not a mind reader."

Sam smiled. "Again, I apologise. I'm often guilty of ploughing on, without thinking first, in my eagerness to solve a grave crime, or three, in this case."

"There's no need for you to apologise, I fully appreciate the stress you must be under to get results for the force these days. My father used to be a serving police officer... I'm talking around forty years ago."

"What rank did he make?" Sam asked.

"He wasn't very ambitious, only ever made it to being a PC on the beat. Even so, he used to come home at night shattered and was always complaining about the cutbacks and that his workload had multiplied considerably, with fewer coppers around. He didn't remain on the beat for long because they did away with that role years ago, as you know. Until his dying day, he always maintained that was the force's downfall and the reason the crime rates in this country rocketed, you know, when they ditched the bobbies on the beat.

Bobbies, there you go, I'm showing my age again, even your partner frowned at that one."

Sam glanced at Bob who shrugged.

"I've heard of it, only last week in fact, during a quiz show," Bob admitted.

Suppressing a smile, Sam returned her attention to Hamilton. "I fear you could be right. Do you know the other FAs well, or are you too competitive for customers to get on with them?"

"Not at all, it's not like that in our line of business. I know Denis well enough, we've even met up for lunch a few times in the past, not often. Phil is a different kettle of fish entirely. I wouldn't say he's a law unto himself, but you get my meaning when I say that, don't you?"

"I do. Have you ever had any problems, professionally, with either one of them?"

"Not as such."

"Have any of your customers come to you after being ill-advised by either of the other two?"

"All the time. In fairness, that's more likely to be because the markets have been somewhat volatile, rather than the advice they've given. Investing large sums of money isn't for the faint-hearted. You need nerves of steel. You will never make back your money overnight. We advise people to lock as much away as they can afford without leaving themselves destitute. It's always advisable to keep a few thousand in the bank for emergencies. Let's face it, none of us know what lies around the corner, do we?"

Sam nodded. "That much is true, as our three victims would attest to, if they were still with us."

"Are you telling me you believe there's a specific connection between the three crimes and it's to do with the advice they've been given about their investments?"

Sam raised a finger. "That's what we're unsure of at this

stage. There is a substantial link between the victims that we're not willing to ignore, hence our enquiries today."

"Goodness me. I've never heard the like in all my years of trading in this business, which, let me tell you, are considerable. And I'm assuming these victims invested in the three companies which you referred to at the beginning of our conversation, is that right?"

Sam inwardly cringed. It was difficult not revealing all the evidence in a case such as this, when there was an obvious connection and they had the tough job of finding the link that could put the killer away. "Sadly, yes. I've given you more information than intended. I'm going to have to ask you to keep what I've told you to yourself, until an arrest has been made."

He leaned back and threaded his fingers together over his bloated stomach. "Well, I suppose this day had to come, what with the current climate, everyone is trying to make ends meet... That came out wrong, I didn't mean to imply that I'm condoning killing off one's clients, I'm not, far from it. But everyone is struggling under this government, especially in my line of business. People don't have the savings these days to put away for long periods, at least, that's what I'm seeing. It's been that way for a while under the Tories. But we won't get into the politics of it all. This country is in a shambles at present."

"It is, however, that doesn't give someone the right to rob people blind and then come back to kill them a few months later."

He gasped. "Is that what we're talking about here? Jesus, what a nerve."

Sam mentally kicked herself again for allowing her tongue to run away from her. "If there's nothing further you can add, we're going to leave it there for today. I'll give you one of my cards, in the hope that if you think of anything else we should know you contact me ASAP. We're dealing with some of the worst crimes this town has ever had to deal with. Please, I can't emphasise enough the need to keep quiet about anything you've heard today."

He sat upright, exuding his professionalism. "You have my word, Inspector. I hope you find the person you're looking for."

Sam and Bob rose from their seats.

"Thank you," Sam said, "so do we."

They left the office and walked back to the car.

"That was unusual, even for you," Bob said after taking a few steps.

She briefly closed her eyes and then opened them again, dreading the looming conversation she sensed they were about to embark upon. "Go on, say it. You think I've divulged too much and he's going to be in there now, sitting at his desk, calling the other FAs in the area."

"I wouldn't necessarily put it that way. What's eating you?"

"I know I overstepped the mark in my eagerness to capture the killer. I bit down on my tongue more times than I care to think about back there."

"It happens. You're passionate about finding the culprit. In fairness, once you started asking about these false companies it became obvious, even to me, what you were getting at. You're beating yourself up for no reason. This is one of those cases where it's impossible to disguise the truth and reality behind what has happened."

Sam stopped and turned to face him. "Thanks, Bob, I needed to hear that."

His cheeks flushed. "Get away with you. You're forgetting what a fantastic detective you are, Sam. Doubting yourself unnecessarily. I have confidence in your ability to find the perpetrator."

"Thanks again, Bob, but we need to find the killer soon, before yet another person loses their life. Here's something that has just dawned on me that I should have thought about before we set off..."

"What's that?"

They continued their walk back to the car.

"That the killer of the last two victims in particular, was a woman, and yet the three FAs in this area are all men."

"Fuck! Why didn't that occur to me when I was making the list? Although the CCTV showed a man and woman in the car."

"Hmm... there is that."

"Is it worth going to see the others?"

"We've come this far, it would be foolish of us to turn back now. Just see it as one more obstacle in our way. We may glean something that piques our interest when we're talking with the others."

"What if it's one of their wives, or partners, who has carried out the murders?"

They reached the car, and Sam glanced over the roof at her partner. "Possibly. We can't rule anything out at this point. Hop in, on to the next one. You have my permission to give me a kick if you sense I'm about to slip up and give too much away."

He raised an eyebrow. "You're kidding me, right?"

"Yes and no. Get in."

THEY ARRIVED at the next location ten minutes later. Sam parked the car behind the building they were after, and they set off to begin their enquiries all over again. This time, she knew she had to restrain herself, as far as the questions she wanted to ask were concerned.

It was a similar setup as the last establishment they had

visited. Two desks, one at the front and the other at the rear. A female with a pointed chin and her hair secured up in a bun on top of her head smiled as they entered. Sam produced her warrant card.

"Is it possible to speak to Phil Bradley?" There was no one else in the room.

"He's indisposed at the moment. Can I help? I'm his assistant."

"Indisposed, as in he's around and not able to see us at the moment or he's elsewhere?"

The assistant grinned, her teeth glistening under the lights. "I meant he's in the loo and shouldn't be too long. Why don't you take a seat? Can I get you a drink while you're waiting? It'll have to be either teabags or instant coffee."

"No, we're fine, thanks all the same."

She smiled again and went back to her work, tapping on her keyboard non-stop until the door opened at the rear of the office. She glanced up at the man in his forties who had entered the room.

"Phil. These people are from the police, they want a word with you."

Phil's eyes darted between his assistant, Sam and Bob. If she didn't know any better, Sam would have said he was about to take flight. Maybe her suspicion gene was playing her up and she was doing the man an injustice.

"I see. And what would the police want with a financial advisor?"

"A quick word, if you have the time?"

He peeked at his watch. "I have a few minutes before my next client is due, how does that sound to you?" He motioned for them to join him at his desk.

"I've got my kicking leg ready," Bob whispered as they made their way to their seats.

Sam jabbed him with her elbow, connecting with his ribs. "I sense this is going to be a tricky one."

"I'm getting the same impression," Bob confirmed.

Sam ensured a smile was set in place as she took her seat. "Thanks for seeing us today. We'll try and make this quick."

"What's this about?"

"We were wondering if you've had any dealings with any of these companies: Secured Capital, Hall's Investments and Romney Finances?" She tried to assess his reaction but struggled. She thought she caught a glimmer of recognition when she mentioned the first company, but perhaps her instinct was awry on that one.

He paused for a moment or two before he responded. "No, none of them are ringing a bell with me. May I ask why?"

Learning from her previous mistake, she swallowed and said, "I can't really go into detail. Would you mind checking your system for me? How many companies do you deal with on a regular basis?"

"Hundreds. However, I can assure you I don't recognise the names at all."

"If you'd check the system for me, all the same, I'd appreciate it."

"Very well. Remind me what the first one was called again."

"Secured Capital."

"Nothing coming up for that name at all. Next was something Investments, what was it?"

"Hall's Investments."

"Ah yes. Again, no, sorry, nothing showing up for that one at all. And the third one was?"

"Romney Finances," Sam replied, her heart sinking with every negative response he gave.

"Let's see. Again, no such luck, I'm afraid. Can I ask what your interest is in these companies?"

"They're connected to an investigation we're working on. I'm afraid I can't offer you more than that."

"Very odd. Is there anything else I can do for you?"

"Yes, you can tell me how well you get on with the other FAs in the area."

"It seems a touch odd to be asking me that. Okay, I suppose. My workload is pretty full-on, so I don't have time to socialise with them, if that's what you're asking."

"But I take it you share resources with them occasionally, yes?"

"Sometimes. I'm an independent FA for a reason, in that I prefer to work alone."

"Have any of your clients ever come to you saying they've been ill-advised or badly treated by either of the other two FAs in Workington?"

"Another strange question. No, I don't recall that ever happening, not really. Of course, you're bound to have a couple of dissatisfied customers come through the door now and again, but nothing that is really standing out. Why? What have the others been up to?"

"We'll leave it there for now. Thanks for all your help today."

With that, a woman in her fifties entered the front door.

He smiled at the woman and left his seat. "If you'll excuse me, that's Mrs Grimshaw now."

"Thanks for squeezing us in. I'm going to leave you my card. Should you think of anything else we might need to know about, please get in touch."

"I'm sure there won't be. I think we've covered everything that needs to be said." He glanced down at the card. "Inspector Cobbs."

"Just in case, sir, you never know."

Sam and Bob left the building and returned to the car.

"Another wasted trip," Bob grumbled.

"Bah humbug. Stop your whining. One left, then we'll call it a day and see if the others have made any headway in our absence."

"Are we taking bets on it?" Bob teased then slipped into the passenger seat.

Sam dived behind the steering wheel. "I'm not in a betting mood. I'm more in an optimistic one that they won't let us down."

"They won't. Something has to give sooner or later."

Sam started the engine. "You'd like to think so, eh? We're coming for you, Mr Denis Knott, whether you like it or not. Remind me of the address again."

Bob set up the satnav, and Sam indicated into the traffic which was building up at this time of day.

CHAPTER 9

he final stop was opposite one of the large supermarkets in the town. They entered the office as an older woman was leaving. There was a man in his late forties sitting at a messy desk and a younger man dealing with an enquiry on the telephone. The older man got to his feet and approached them with a broad smile.

"Hello there. What can we do for you on this cold, damp day?"

Sam returned the smile and held up her warrant card. "DI Sam Cobbs, and this is my partner, DS Bob Jones. We were hoping to have a chat with Denis Knott."

"Oh, that's me. Forgive my confusion, would you mind telling me what this is about?" He glanced over his shoulder at his colleague and saw that the younger man was still busy on the phone and let out a relieved sigh.

"We're conducting enquiries concerning an ongoing investigation we're dealing with."

"What kind of investigation? Are you allowed to tell me, or is it all hush-hush, on a need-to-know basis?" He laughed, but his smile slipped when Sam just stared at him.

"A serious one. A murder inquiry."

His mouth opened and closed, imitating a fish out of water. "Murder! Oh my. My legs have gone weak, I need to sit down."

They followed him through the open office to his desk. He threw himself into his seat and gestured for them to take the weight off their feet, too.

"Thanks. Are you all right?" Sam was forced to ask, sensing the man was a bit of a drama queen.

"I think so. Who? Who has been murdered?"

Sam suspected that this interview was going to consist of him asking far more questions than Sam would, so she decided it would be best to put a stop to that right away. "We don't have much time, not with a killer on the loose, sir. I have several questions I need to ask you. If you'll do me the honour of answering them swiftly, we'll be out of your hair soon enough."

"Of course. If that's the way you want to play it. Ask your first question, and I'll see if I can supply an answer to it."

"I have a list of companies that I need to know if you've ever had any dealings with."

He nodded but remained quiet.

Sam continued, "Secured Capital, Hall's Investments and Romney Finances. Have you either heard of them or worked with any, or all, of the companies?"

"Sorry, I've never heard of them. I can categorically tell you that without the need for me to look it up. I deal with dozens of companies daily but I've never come across any of those. May I ask what the connection is to your murder inquiry?"

"I'll come to that at the end of the interview. What about the other two FAs in the area?"

"You'll have to ask them the same question. I cannot possibly tell you who they have connections with."

"Sorry, I was trying to keep my questions brief and slipped up. What I meant to ask was, how do you get on with the other two FAs operating in Workington?"

He appeared to relax into his chair, and a smile broke out. "Ah, I see now. I've had dealings with James Hamilton over the years, even attended an FA conference with him a few years back, that was being held in London, but that Phil Bradley... well, he gives me the impression that he prefers to keep his cards close to his chest. He probably thinks I'm going to entice his clients away from him. The man always comes across as being very standoffish to me. Although that might be me misreading the signs, because I haven't really had that much to do with him. If that makes sense?"

"It does. So would you say you treat each other as competitors?"

"I suppose so. I would class James as a friend and a business associate as opposed to a competitor."

"Interesting. Is there any specific reason for that? Has Bradley overstepped the mark at all with you?"

"No, not really. It's simply his attitude. Believe me, since he opened his office a few years ago, I've tried to reach out to offer the hand of friendship, only to get it slapped away. I've given up now."

"I can understand your reluctance to keep trying. Have you had any need to be angry with him?"

"Angry? In what way?"

"Because of the way he's dealt with a client?"

"I'm not sure I understand your question, Inspector. How would I know how he deals with his clients when I don't have much to do with him?"

"Sorry, yes, you're right. Perhaps you can tell me if any of your clients came to you after seeking advice from Bradley?"

He contemplated the question for a moment or two, then

nodded. "Yes, there is one lady I can think of in particular. She came here after calling in at his office about a year ago."

Out of the corner of her eye, Sam saw Bob extract his pen and notebook from his pocket. "Care to tell us more?"

"It was a lady by the name of Yvonne Jenkins. I'm not sure if I should tell you the ins and outs because of client confidentiality."

"In that case, I would need to remind you that we're dealing with a murder inquiry here, Mr Knott."

He fidgeted and tapped his keyboard. "Let me bring up her file to refresh my memory. Ah, here it is. Mrs Jenkins had sadly lost her husband a few months before she came seeking advice about investments. She told me that she'd called at Bradley's office the week before but had picked up bad vibes about him."

"Bad vibes?"

"I didn't push her on the subject, it's not my job to show any kind of disrespect to 'a competitor', that's not the way I work. I tend to bend over backwards for my clients, make them feel cherished, that's how I've managed to keep trading for the last fifteen years or so."

"Glad to hear it. A client would need to feel they trusted you if they're considering putting their life savings into your hands."

"That's my point exactly. This lady felt pressured by Bradley to invest her money with him, at least that's what she hinted at when she was sat in that chair."

"Hinted at? So she didn't come out and tell you what actually happened?"

"No, you'd really need to ask her that question."

"Can you supply her address for me, rather than me having to contact the station and put in a request?"

"Providing you don't tell her that I gave it to you."

"Sounds okay to me."

154

He proceeded to tap more keys, and then the printer churned into life in the corner. Knott left his seat and collected the piece of paper. He handed it to Sam. "There you go. Look, I treat my clients as kings and queens as soon as they step through that front door. If Bradley treats his clients the way he's treated me over the years when I've tried to reach out, then yes, he's bound to put clients off. Maybe Mrs Jenkins will be able to go into more detail for you on that front. Was there anything else?"

Sam waved the sheet of paper and smiled. "I think that's all for now. I'm going to leave you my card. If you happen to think of anything else I should know, will you get in touch?"

"You've got it. I've always been willing to work with the police over the years."

He saw Sam and Bob to the front door.

"Thanks for all your help," Sam said. She shook the man's hand.

He smiled. "It's a shame you didn't trust me enough to fill me in on the details of the investigation."

"If only we had time on our side. We really do appreciate the information you've supplied."

"My pleasure. I hope you find the person you're looking for, Inspector."

Bob closed the door behind them. "I take it we're going to call in and see what this Mrs Jenkins has to say next?"

"We are. Do you have a problem with that, Bob?"

"No, it was a simple question."

THE HOUSE WAS one of the grandest houses that Sam had ever come across. The drive was long and sweeping. The entrance porch was made of oak, and the thatched roof added to the charm of the property.

"Stunning," Sam whispered as she got out of the car.

"There's a pretty penny tied up in this place, that's for sure," Bob admitted.

Sam was surprised his assessment hadn't been accompanied by a whistle.

"Definitely. Let's see what she has to say about her experience with Phil Bradley."

The bell was a wrought-iron pull in the shape of a twisted Gaelic knot. After the bell sounded, it seemed like a lifetime before the door was opened by a lady in her seventies.

Sam flashed her warrant card. "Hello, Mrs Jenkins, I'm DI Sam Cobbs of the Cumbria Constabulary. Would it be possible for us to come in and speak with you for a moment or two?"

She eyed them both cautiously. "Does he have a name, too?" she asked, her gaze landing on Bob.

"Sorry, yes. This is my partner, DS Bob Jones. Forgive my rudeness, I should have mentioned it."

"Yes, you should have. Very well, you'd better come in."

Sam cringed, getting off on the wrong foot with the woman. She allowed them to enter the vast hallway and then closed the behind them with a large bang. The noise echoed around the interior of the grand home.

"Why are you here? There has never before been a reason for me to be visited by the police. You have piqued my interest with your arrival."

Sam smiled despite the absence of one on Mrs Jenkins' lined face. "We were hoping you could give us some details about one of the financial advisors in the area. Or should I say your experience with one in particular."

A deep frown caused even more wrinkles to form on her brow. "What on earth are you talking about? You're going to need to be more succinct with your questions, Inspector. It's too cold to discuss this out here, I have a wood burner alight in the lounge, why don't we go in there?"

"That would be wonderful, if you're sure we're not putting you out at all."

"You are, but that's a different story. I'm cold out here and I need to be wary about my health."

She led the way into a vast room. To one end was a library, in the middle was a dining area, and in front of them was a cosy lounge. All the seating surrounded the roaring wood burner, not a TV in sight.

"Please, take a seat, anywhere but the armchair closest to the fire, that has my name on it."

"You have a beautiful home, Mrs Jenkins. Have you lived here long?"

"Over forty years, and thank you. Now, you haven't come here to discuss my home, you mentioned something about FAs in the area. What about them, and who are you talking about in particular?" She placed her interlocked hands in her lap, resting them on her plaid woollen skirt.

"If I said the name Phil Bradley, would you know who I was talking about?"

"I would. What's he been up to? No doubt something dodgy, otherwise you wouldn't be knocking on my door, would you?"

"We're making general enquiries at the moment, and another financial advisor in the area mentioned that you had chosen to deal with him rather than Mr Bradley. I hope I haven't put my foot in it."

"Why on earth should my name crop up in a conversation with the police? I'm perplexed about this."

"I'm sorry, there's no need for you to be. We were making enquiries with Mr Knott, asking him if he'd ever had any customers come to him via Mr Bradley, and your name was mentioned."

"I'm far from happy about this. I'll be having a word with Mr Knott in the not too distant future."

"Honestly, only your name was mentioned, he refused to divulge anything further, especially about your finances."

"I should hope not," she replied stiffly. "You put your trust in these people, and this is how they repay you. I think it's appalling that my name cropped up at all."

Sam inwardly heaved on a sigh she was determined to suppress. "Please don't be mad at him. It was during our interview that I asked if any of his customers had been treated harshly by Mr Bradley. You were the only person he could think of. If anything, I forced your details out of him. Please allow me to clarify. I'm the lead investigator in a triple murder inquiry."

Mrs Jenkins held up a hand to prevent Sam from saying anything else. "Am I to understand that you believe a financial advisor is behind these murders?"

"There's a grave possibility that's the case, yes. Therefore, I'm sure you can understand our urgency to come here today and find out a few facts about your business dealings with Mr Bradley."

"I'm not sure I do. I'm distraught to think that my name is possibly linked to a murder inquiry, whether you regard it on the periphery or not. To my ears, all I'm hearing is Yvonne Jenkins, Bradley, Knott and a murder inquiry. My goodness, I never thought I'd live to see this day. I have to add, I have never once been in trouble with the police before. I'm mortified, simply mortified, to have you show up here on my doorstep."

"I'm so sorry. It wasn't my intention to come here and upset you like this. Please, we're simply making general enquiries into a person of interest who has recently come to our attention."

Mrs Jenkins's breathing became heavy. Her chest rose and fell significantly as Sam assessed her appearance.

"Are you okay?"

"I'm angry, that's all. My health hasn't been the best since my husband departed, but what I'm feeling now has nothing to do with that."

"Okay. Am I all right to continue?"

"Yes, please do. I'll try and be of assistance if I can. The sooner I get you out of my house the better, no offence intended."

Sam smiled. "I'd probably feel the same if I were in your shoes."

"Good, now we have an understanding between us. Ask what you need to ask so I can get on with enjoying my peaceful day. I don't get many of them as it is, what with being involved with different clubs and societies."

"We won't take up much of your time, I promise. Is it possible for you to go over what happened when you visited Mr Bradley's office?"

"Well, I have to say, at first, I liked the man. He seemed quite reserved, a quiet disposition, and I was all ready to do business with him."

"What changed?"

"He did. Once he found out how much I was willing to invest with him."

Sam frowned. "Can you explain how?"

"It's obvious that I'm a wealthy woman, you only have to look around you to see that, don't you?"

Sam nodded.

"Well, when my husband died, all his shares came my way, and the other property we owned. My daughter was well catered for in the Will, and she will inherit the rest of what I have once I depart this world, so she insisted I go on a world cruise and invest a large pot of the money. When I ran this scenario past Bradley, he flipped, told me I was being irresponsible and that every penny I had should be tied up rather than me going out there spending the money on enjoying myself. As you can imagine, I was affronted by not only his tone but also his advice. He had no right telling me what I can and can't do with my money, no one has. I walked out of there, disinterested in the advice he had to offer, and went elsewhere, to Denis Knott. He did everything he could to make me feel welcome. Advised me that I shouldn't tie up all my money in stocks and shares and at my time of life I should be out there, going on mini adventures, enjoying myself. I liked him, so decided to give him my business and haven't regretted my decision, up until now."

"I'm sorry you think that way, he didn't mean to break any confidences. All he was trying to do was help with our enquiries. Please don't punish him for doing the right thing."

"That remains to be seen. I will be having a serious word in his ear once you leave today. Was there anything else?"

"Perhaps you can tell me if Bradley mentioned putting the money away with a certain company?"

"Gosh, this was a few months ago now, I'm not sure I can summon up the name on a whim. Give me a moment to think about that."

"We're not in a rush."

"I've got part of it, I think. Something Finances. I know that's probably no help, especially when speaking about a financial advisor."

"What about Romney Finances, does that sound familiar?"

Mrs Jenkins smiled and nodded. "That's the one. Yes, that's definitely the one he spoke about. He was very eager for me to invest with them. How did you know?"

"The company name has surfaced during our investigation."

"Oh my, as a fraudulent one? I had a gut feeling that it was the wrong move to make."

"It's a perplexing one, the company no longer exists. We can't say any more than that just now because we simply haven't got any further details. My team are working day and night to find out more about the company and why it went bust."

Mrs Jenkins exhaled a relieved breath. "My goodness, I've come over all strange. What if I had trusted that man with my life savings? My daughter's inheritance? That man should be shut down, no longer be trading. Gosh, it's as if he knew the business was about to fold, the way he was pushing me to invest with them."

"We'll look into it further. I can't thank you enough for being brutally honest with us today. I'm sorry if we've caused you any unnecessary anxiety, that truly wasn't our intention."

"It's forgotten about. I'm so relieved I didn't go with him and ended up putting my faith in Knott instead. My investments had been doing well up until that confounded woman took over our country and... well, the less said about that the better. The markets seem to have recovered a little under the new PM. Mind you, I don't think they'll be in power for long, do you?"

"I'm afraid I have very little interest in politics."

"That's the trouble with the younger generation, you should do. Casting your vote can make a world of difference to not just who becomes our next Prime Minister but also to the economy and to the amount you have in your pocket at the end of the day."

"If I didn't realise that before, I definitely do now, after what we've been through as a nation over this past winter. Thank you for allowing us into your home today and for taking the time to explain your experience. We won't delay you any longer."

Sam and Bob left their seats.

Mrs Jenkins showed them back into the hallway and opened the front door for them. "I'm sorry for my behaviour towards you both. It's the unknown that clouded my judgement."

"There's really no need for you to apologise. Thank you for sparing the time to speak with us. Enjoy the rest of your day."

"I'll try. Goodbye."

On the way to the car, Bob was surprisingly quiet.

"What did you make of that?" Sam asked.

"I'm still considering it," he replied before he jumped into the car.

"I don't want to rock the boat too soon. I need more evidence to back up our suspicions about Bradley first."

"Always wise to go with the evidence. There's also the small detail of the killer being a woman to overcome as well."

Sam tutted. "You're right. Let's get back to the station and see what we can find out about Bradley. We might be dealing with another double act of serial killers."

"Joy of joys, something to get excited about after the last couple we encountered. Maybe it's a new sexual experience."

Sam shot a look in his direction. "A what?"

"You know, maybe these psychos get off on it... kill someone then make out somewhere, probably down a back alley in the car."

"Should I be worried about your knowledge of such matters, partner?"

"Bollocks. I'm surmising, that's what detectives do, right? Come up with a plausible plan or two, or three. I'm still waiting for possible alternatives that you might want to offer."

"You'll be waiting a long time then, Bob. I'd rather deal in facts not supposition, you should be aware of that by now."

"You blow hot and cold, alter your mind more often than I change my underwear."

Sam burst into laughter. "You crack me up. And by the way, that was too much information for my liking."

"Them's the breaks."

CHAPTER 10

Claire was wearing a huge smile the second Sam and Bob entered the incident room.

Sam was immediately drawn to her desk to see what the heck was going on. "I take it you have some good news for us, Claire?"

"You could say that, boss." She handed Sam an A4 piece of paper.

Sam swiftly cast her eyes over it. "This is what we've been waiting for. Let's go through it as a team. Bob, will you get everyone a coffee?"

"Do I have to?" By now he was relaxing in his chair.

Claire left her seat and headed for the drinks station instead. "I'll get them."

"Maybe I should switch partners," Sam hissed, glaring at Bob whose mouth had dropped open. She faced the white-board and jotted down the relevant information that Claire had gathered in their absence.

Claire distributed the coffees, and the team pulled their seats into a semi-circle.

"Who are those people?" Bob enquired.

"You'll find out when the others do. Everyone settled into position?" Sam spotted Alex still at his desk, scribbling something in his notebook.

"Two secs, and I'll be with you, boss."

"In your own time, Alex, I've got all day."

He joined them moments later and gave Sam an apologetic smile. "Sorry."

She accepted his apology with a nod and moved on. "Okay, this is what we have, thanks to Claire and her contact in the Fraud Squad."

"Good old Claire," Bob mumbled.

Sam glanced at Claire who chuckled and shrugged. She shook her head, telling Sam to ignore him. Sam would deal with him later, his attitude of late sucked.

"As I was saying, the information we've been given, could, I think, be pivotal to our investigation. I've listed three names on the board: Dana Powell, Jennifer Moriarty and Sheila Bradley. One name, at least the surname, is of particular interest, and that's Sheila Bradley, bearing in mind the fact that Bob and I have just returned from visiting all the FAs, one of whom was Phil Bradley."

"His wife? Part of the serial killer team?" Bob suggested.

"It would be wrong of us to dismiss that idea. But what about the other two women?"

"What's the connection? You haven't spilled the relevance behind each of the names," Bob said.

"The three ladies in question are listed as the directors or owners of the companies that went bust," Sam filled in.

"Do you need us to do the background checks on each of them, boss?" Alex asked, his pen poised.

"I think we should. First, I'll give you a brief rundown of what took place when we visited the FAs today." She spent the next five minutes going over the details.

"So, what you're telling us is that you believe Phil Bradley is behind the murders?" Oliver asked.

"I'm not sure if he's the main culprit or not, because we've been led to believe that two of the murders involved a woman, possibly the same woman, showing up at the victims' homes," Sam replied.

"You have a gut instinct that Bradley is involved but we need to find out in what capacity, is that right?" Claire asked.

"Correct. Let's see if we can trace these women back to Bradley." She faced the board and circled one of the names, that of Sheila Bradley. "I can't see this name being a coincidence, can you? During the background checks carried out on Phil Bradley, has this woman's name surfaced at all?"

Suzanna nodded. "I was about to mention that her name has already cropped up in a search. She's his ex-wife."

Sam's heart sank. "How long since they got divorced?"

"Around ten months ago," Suzanna confirmed. "She's still listed as being the owner of the marital home, if that helps?"

"It does. Bob and I will shoot over there now, see where the land lies and ask the question as to why her name is listed as a company director on a business that has folded. Wait, do we know if she worked for the company? If so, that would explain why, wouldn't it?"

Suzanna checked her notebook and said, "Nope, as far as I know she's never worked alongside her husband."

"Interesting. While we're out, if you can, do the necessary research into the other two names, let's see if we can get this all wrapped up by the end of the day. It's three-fifteen now, so it's pushing it, but do your best for me, peeps."

Chairs scraped, and the team returned to their desks. Bob slipped his jacket back on and seemed reluctant to set off again.

"Everything all right?" Sam asked, eager to get on the road.

"I need to nip to the loo first. Have I got time or will I be holding you up?"

"Cut the crap, Bob. In fact, I'll join you."

His eyes widened in shock.

"I meant I'll go to the ladies' while you shake your manhood in the gents'."

Again, he appeared lost for words, and a snarky rebuttal failed to materialise.

She sniggered behind his back as they left the incident room.

They went their separate ways, and she called over her shoulder, "Don't forget to sing 'Happy Birthday' while you're washing your hands."

He growled and barged into the toilets without responding.

Sam did the necessary in the cubicle and washed her hands. She stared at her reflection, noting how pale and drawn she looked. "Not long to go now, stick with it, girl."

She found Bob scrolling through his phone on the landing. "You took your time."

"I sang two verses of 'Happy Birthday' while I cleaned up."

She smiled and descended the stairs ahead of him. "Figures, you always have to go the extra mile, don't you?"

THE HOUSE WAS out in the country on the edge of Workington. It was a detached home with a large garden at the front. In the fading light, Sam caught a glimpse of the size of the back garden and the fields beyond. To her, this would be a dream location to settle down with Rhys and Sonny and any other dogs that might come along in the future. Sitting in the small drive, over to the left, in front of the double garage, was a sleek black Audi sports car.

"Nice motor," Bob announced.

"With a matching nice house. Let's hope she's in, if the car is here." Sam rang the doorbell and turned to admire the tidiness of the front garden. A few early daffodils had sprung up but hadn't opened yet at the front of the border, nature's way of letting her know that the winter had been mild despite what Sam had thought.

A chain was removed from the door, and it swung open. Sam dipped her hand in her pocket to retrieve her warrant card.

"Hi, can I help?" The woman was in her forties, dyed blonde hair and very slim in her jeans.

"Hello, Mrs Bradley. I'm DI Sam Cobbs, and this is my partner, DS Bob Jones. Would it be all right if we came in and spoke with you for a moment or two?"

"Oh, the police. You're not coming in until you tell me what this is all about, plus I'll need to verify your identities. I'm very wary about strangers knocking at my door these days."

"Of course. I'll give you my warrant card. Do you have the number of the station to hand?"

"I'll look it up. Give me a few minutes, providing the station answers promptly." She closed the door before Sam could respond.

"Great. Meanwhile, we're stuck out here in this dreary weather with the wind howling against our backs," Bob complained.

"You do bloody exaggerate. There's a slight breeze, and that's only because we're high up around here."

Not long after, the door opened again, and Mrs Bradley swept an arm in front of her, inviting them in.

"Shoes on or off?" Sam asked.

"Whatever, makes no odds to me. You didn't tell me why you're here. Have I broken the law in some way?"

"Possibly. Can we go somewhere more comfortable?" Sam asked.

"What? There has to be some mistake... I've never done anything illegal, never. Come into the lounge, I've just lit the fire."

They entered the lounge to find a clump of logs burning in the open grate. There was nothing like an open fire for adding instant cosiness to the room, even if they were less efficient than a wood-burning stove, in Sam's opinion.

"Please, take a seat. My nerves are shot to pieces, you being here. I have no idea what I've done. If I've broken the law then it must have been by mistake, you have to believe me."

"There's no need for you to worry, at least I don't think there is. Have you ever heard of a company called Secured Capital?"

She scratched the side of her face, and her brow knitted. "No. Should I have?"

"Something has come to our attention today, while dealing with an investigation, that we find perplexing."

"I don't understand. What type of investigation?"

"We're dealing with a murder inquiry."

"What? And that has led you to my door? I find this incredible, hard to believe or even understand. It sounds like something my ex would know about, not me. He's a financial advisor."

"We know, we've already interviewed him."

"What? And he put my name forward? How bloody dare he? There's a reason I divorced that shithead. I have no regrets on that score."

"No, he didn't lead us here as such. We've carried out some research into companies that have gone bust in the area, and Secured Capital came to our attention."

"I must be thick, I'm still not grasping what any of this has to do with me."

Sam smiled, hoping to keep the woman on her side and cut through her mounting anxiety. "Please, hear me out. Our research has shown that when this company went bust sometime last year, you were named as a director."

Mrs Bradley leapt to her feet. "I what? That's impossible. I demand to know what's going on here."

"Please, take a seat, Mrs Bradley."

She threw herself back into her chair and shuffled to the edge, then clenched her hands together. "Call me Sheila, I'm in the process of ditching his name. My solicitor is on the slow side."

"Sheila, as I said, your name was registered as a director. Are you telling me you've never had any dealings with this company?"

"No, yes, I mean, never. This is the first I'm hearing about it. I'm in shock, can't you tell? And no, this is not me acting, this is me genuinely shocked. What is going on here? I'm totally confused."

"Could your husband have used your identity to start up the business?"

She sighed and nodded. "I wouldn't put it past him. Come the end of our marriage, he was a total stranger to me. Gone was the man I married all those years ago. He was someone you loved to be with, friendly, outgoing, and an all-round nice guy."

"What changed him?"

Sheila's gaze dropped to her hands. "His mother died, and he started gambling. It tore our marriage apart, his addiction. He was so close to his mother; growing up it was just the two of them when she left his abusive father. He was so grateful to her for getting them both out of the house. She lived with us, come the end, before her death. Alzheimer's claimed her mind, and there was no going back. The deterioration happened swiftly, unlike others who have to deal with the disease and all it throws at them and their families for years. Our torture was over within a few months. It crucified Phil, though. He never admitted it, but I always got the impression he blamed me for her death. I was the one stuck at home, day in day out, caring for all her needs, while he went off to work."

"That must have been horrendous for both of you."

"When the day came that she took her last breath, he left the house and didn't return for three days."

"Where did he go?"

"He visited every casino he could find within a fifty-mile radius and lost a fortune. I was frantic, didn't sleep for days. Constantly rang all the hospitals within Cumbria to see if he had been admitted. Nothing. Suddenly, he showed up on the third day, full of remorse. I felt sorry for him, it was clear his mother's death had taken its toll on him, on both of us. It wasn't until the credit card statements arrived at the end of the month that I started putting two and two together and realised he'd lost all of our savings and more. I kicked him out of the family home, this home. I've had to return to work; fortunately, my PA skills were still up to scratch, and I found a top job with a local businessman. He's away at a meeting for a few days, hence me being at home. He told me to take a couple of days off, so I jumped at the chance. I was enjoying my break, too, until you showed up." She launched a glimmer of a smile before it quickly dispersed. "He must have forged my signature."

"You think? Would he sink that low?"

"He's addicted to gambling. If he needed to pay off his debts, then yes, I'd say he would sink that low, wouldn't you?"

"Possibly. Any idea of the amount of debt we're talking about here?"

"That first credit card statement highlighted it ran into tens of thousands. I was both shocked and appalled he could treat me like that. I thought I knew that man inside and out. How wrong I was." She shuddered. "Why do men change so much when the chips are down? Why do they have problems solving issues relating to money? Why is it always down to the women to sort out?"

Sam sighed. "Sadly, that's true for many men. I had the same with my husband." Sam bit down on her tongue for allowing her private circumstances to interfere with her professional life. "Ignore me, I shouldn't have mentioned that."

"I'm sorry you had to go through a similar situation. Did you leave him? Are you still together after working through your issues? Oh no, you don't have to answer, I should never have asked."

"Unfortunately, my husband committed suicide... not long ago. We were separated at the time."

Sheila gasped, and her hand clasped her mouth. After a few seconds of staring at Sam, she dropped her hand into her lap. "I'm so sorry. I knew it was insensitive of me to ask."

"It wasn't, don't worry about it. I'm getting stronger every day. Anyway, this visit isn't about me. It's clear that you had no knowledge of this company, therefore, I'm prepared to let the matter lie. If you'll do one thing for me in exchange?"

"Oh my, anything. What do you need?"

"Will you give us a statement to the effect that you've never heard of this company? Also, give us the details of your husband's, sorry, ex-husband's debts."

"Of course I will. I know you believe me, but is there any reason for me to be concerned that this could come down on my head in the future?"

"No, I'll make sure of that. It's clear that Mr Bradley has fallen on hard times and is doing everything he can to find a way of paying off the debts he's incurred. Do you happen to know if he's still gambling?"

"I believe so. I saw him a few months ago, he was driving a beat-up old car. I'm presuming he sold his Mercedes, which he thought the world of. Still, that's his problem now, not mine."

"Did his mother leave him any money in her Will?"

"A couple of hundred thousand. It went overnight, at the casinos. How could he? We had a substantial mortgage on this place to consider, hence my need to go back to work. I'm doing okay by myself, there's no need for you to be worried about that. But when you've devoted half your life to being married to a man and his character changes at a snap of your fingers, it's an extremely hard pill to swallow, I can assure you."

"I can imagine. I'm sorry you've had a tough year. We're going to leave now. Would it be all right if I send a uniformed officer to take down your statement?"

"No problem. Will they ring first?"

"Yes. I'll need your number."

Sam jotted it down in her notebook and slipped it back in her pocket. She and Bob followed Sheila back to the front door.

"I know I can trust you to keep this information to yourself."

Sheila nodded. "Oh, you can. I swear you can."

Sam opened the front door and paused to glance over her shoulder at the woman. "We're dealing with three murders. All the victims have had vast amounts of money go missing from their bank accounts."

"What the...? Oh heck, and you believe that Phil is behind these murders?"

Sam waved her hand from side to side. "All the signs are there. What we need to do now is put all the pieces of the puzzle together."

"I don't envy you. Please don't hesitate to get in touch if you think I can be of further assistance."

"That's very kind of you to offer. I'll take you up on that, if the need arises. Needless to say, I'm going to have to ask you to keep the information I've given you today, private. Please do not contact Phil, under any circumstances. We need to build a case against him first before we can bring him in for questioning. What you've told us today has given us a huge insight into what's going on with him and given us a motive for the crimes."

"Goodness me." Sheila visibly shuddered once more. "Just when you think you know someone and he goes and does this... Well, I hope he pays a huge price for what he's done."

An intriguing thought entered Sam's mind. "One last thing... You said his mother's death came on suddenly. Do you believe he could have possibly killed her... to get his hands on her estate?"

"Jesus, that thought has never crossed my mind. The day she died, I was out shopping with a friend of mine. We returned home late that afternoon to find him sobbing by her bed."

Sam sighed. "Convenient. I'll get the pathologist to go over the notes regarding her death, see if there was anything suspicious there."

"I hope you're wrong. He took a rare day off work, forced me to go out, have some time to myself for a change."

Sam raised an eyebrow and left the house.

"Jesus, the plot thickens, eh?" Bob remarked on the way back to the car.

"I've got a distasteful knot in my stomach about this guy.

Wait, I need to ask her something else." Sam jogged back to the house and rang the bell.

Sheila opened the door after a few seconds. "Oh, hello again. Did you forget something?"

"I did. Along with your name, two other names have come to our attention regarding other possible fake companies. If I ran the names past you, would you tell me if you recognise them?"

"Go for it."

"Jennifer Moriarty and Dana Powell."

"Dana definitely. She used to work for Phil. She left suddenly sometime last year."

"That's brilliant, and the other name doesn't mean anything to you?"

"Nothing at all. Sorry."

"There's no need for you to apologise. You've been amazing today. Good luck for the future. Don't let what's happened with Phil sour your chance for happiness."

Sheila smiled. "I take it you've already found someone else?"

"Yes. My husband and I were separated for a few months before I started seeing my new beau. My husband killed himself because I refused to take him back. He's the one who did the dirty on me initially, and yes, he saddled me with a bunch of debts I'm still paying off."

"How terrible. I'm glad you've found someone else and that your bad experience with your husband didn't put you off." Her cheeks flushed crimson. "As it happens, I have a date this evening with someone who works in the same office block as me."

"That's wonderful to hear. Enjoy yourself. Try not to let what has happened today get in the way of you having fun."

"I won't. Thank you for the reassuring words, Inspector. I

hope you nail that son of a bitch ex-husband of mine. I can't get over the fact that he might have killed his own mother."

"Let's put that on hold for the moment. Someone from the station will be in touch soon."

"Thank you."

Sam waved and ran back to the car.

"What was that all about?" Bob asked. "Giving her dating advice, were you?"

"No, not in the slightest. I went back to ask her if she knew the other two women, Jennifer and Dana. She hadn't come across the first one, but apparently, up until sometime last year, Dana used to work for Phil."

"Did she now? I guess that's going to be our next stop, right?"

"Absolutely. We might as well strike while the iron is hot as my father always says."

"He talks a lot of sense, that father of yours."

"I'll pass the compliment on to him."

THEY ARRIVED at Dana Powell's terraced house, situated on a small estate on the edge of the other side of town. The time was fast approaching five p.m.

"What if she's not home from work yet?" Bob asked.

"Then we'll have to call back."

They approached the house and noted a woman in a suit coming down the street towards them. Sam held back from ringing the bell long enough to see the woman walk past them, her hopes dashed.

Bob rang the bell instead. Sam dipped her hand into her coat pocket ready to show her warrant card. However, the door remained unanswered. Sam knocked on the neighbour's door, and a young woman with flushed cheeks and messed-up blonde hair answered it.

"Hi, sorry to trouble you. We wondered if you could tell us what time your neighbour gets home from work."

"Which one? In case you haven't noticed, I have two." The woman grinned.

"Sorry, this house. We're after Dana Powell."

"Ah, okay. Well, you're in luck, I think she finishes at around five. She shouldn't be too long, she works around the corner at the estate agent's. They shut at five."

"Thanks, we'll wait in the car."

"Whatever. I'll get back to sorting out my kids' dinners now, then."

"Good luck with that."

Sam smiled, and the woman tutted.

THEY WAITED in the car for another ten minutes until a young woman in her thirties inserted a key in the front door. Sam and Bob took that as their cue to approach her.

"Dana Powell?"

The woman spun around, her hand flattened over her breast. "Jesus, you scared the crap out of me. Yes, who are you?"

"I apologise. We've been waiting for you to get home. We're DI Sam Cobbs and DS Bob Jones. Would it be convenient if we came inside to speak with you?"

"Do I have a choice?" she asked, eyeing them cautiously.

"Of course you do. You could always accompany us to the station, we could conduct the interview there. It's up to you," Sam stated in a no-nonsense tone.

"It must be serious if you're threatening me. You'd better come in."

"Just for the record, I wouldn't want us to get off on the wrong foot, I wasn't threatening you, I was merely pointing out the options available to you."

"Thank you. You'll need to take your shoes off. I've had new flooring laid throughout a few weeks ago."

"It's not a problem."

Dana entered the house first, paused, removed her shoes, and then walked to the bottom of the stairs, giving Sam and Bob room in the narrow, short hallway to remove their boots and shoes.

"Come through to the kitchen, I'll make you a drink. If you don't want one, that's fine by me. I need one after the fraught day I've had at work."

"Tough days are a pain in the rear. Your neighbour told us you work at a local estate agency."

"That's right." She filled the kettle, invited them to take a seat at the round pine kitchen table, and then folded her arms. "Now, are you going to tell me what this is all about?"

"I'm in charge of an investigation, and we're out and about conducting enquiries."

"That hasn't told me much. About what?"

"Are we to understand that you used to work for Phil Bradley?"

Dana closed her eyes and shook her head. "I'd rather forget about the time I spent working for that man."

Sam's interest mounted. "May I ask why?"

The kettle must have been a rapid boil type because it clicked off not long after. "Tea or coffee?"

"Two coffees, white with one sugar, please."

The woman added the necessary ingredients to the mugs and filled them with water. She carried the drinks to the table and pulled out the chair opposite Sam. Holding the mug in both hands, she stared at it for a moment or two and then sighed. "He turned out to be like every other man I've ever worked for. Vile."

"I'm sorry to hear that. Can you explain what you mean by that statement?"

"The job always starts off well. I have a laugh with my employers, but then... after a while, they always seem to think they have the right to touch you up, to be over-friendly towards you. They make me shudder."

"I'm sorry you had to go through such an ordeal. Is that why you left?"

"Yes. I couldn't stand it any longer. He was married, for God's sake. That's the only reason I started working there because I thought I was safe. Wrong. If anything, he turned out to be far worse than any of the other men I've worked with, who felt they were entitled to grope my arse or my tits, come to that. What gives them the damn right to treat women as sex objects or playthings? It's beyond me. I'm so glad I work with an all-women team nowadays, it makes my working day far more relaxed. Well, when I say that, I mean, all I have to do now is deal with the pressures of everyday life at work, without having to cope with the added stress of keeping a boss's hands off me."

"Did you fall out with Phil over this matter whilst working for him or did you jack in the job and walk out the second he laid his hands on you?"

"It happened briefly a few times. You know the type of thing, he reached across me and his arm brushed against my boob. When I shifted back, he appeared to be suitably embarrassed. It was another couple of weeks before he tried it on again with me. That time it was a full-on grope of my arse. I smacked him around the face. Told him in no uncertain terms that I was there to carry out my job and not to be touched up every second of the day. I started looking for another job that day. It was tough to handle, being the only one in the office with him. Maybe he thought that gave him the right to try it on with me."

"It sounds awful. I've never been put in that position myself but I can imagine how uncomfortable a woman might feel to be put in such an awkward situation. How did he react when you handed in your notice?"

"I didn't. I worked my final day then walked out. I had my other job lined up so I wasn't out of work for long, just took a week's break between. The last day I was there he tried it on with me again. I found the courage to slap him down, had a blazing row with him, pointed out how wrong he was to try and keep taking advantage of me when I had rejected him numerous times already."

"And how did he react?"

"He was utterly shocked as if he didn't know what I was sodding referring to. He's such a prick. I heard his wife kicked him out not long after, no idea what that was about. I'm glad she finally saw sense, he's gross. When you're forced to spend time alone with him... well, he used to make my skin crawl, all day and every day."

"I'm glad you finally plucked up the courage to find a way out and that it has all worked out for you."

"Thanks. Hang on, you mentioned you're here making enquiries with regard to an investigation. Don't tell me the police have finally caught up with him?" Dana chewed on her lip and glanced down at her mug.

Sam didn't immediately jump at Dana's words, instead, she bided her time and took a sip from her coffee. Dana's eyes remained focused on the mug she was holding.

"Care to tell us what you're hinting at Dana?"

"He's dodgy, always has been. I regret the day I ever started working there, the leads I made for him over the phone. It was like I enticed those women into his web, and that's when he swooped."

Sam tilted her head. "I'm not sure I understand what you're saying."

"I nearly came down the station to make the police aware of what he was up to. When I stopped working for him, I toyed with the idea continuously, had numerous sleepless nights, but then decided that it would probably backfire on me if I said anything."

"Said anything about what?"

"The companies he was setting up. Illegal companies to get these women, and some men even, to put their money into. Dodgy investments, all the time he robbed the pot... God, I hope I haven't talked myself into trouble now. I got out when I could, I promise you."

"You're telling me that you were aware that he was creating these fake businesses and allowed it to continue?"

Her head bowed, her chin hitting her chest. "I'm sorry. He gave me a bonus. Every time he set up a new business and closed it down again. Thinking about it now, it was probably to keep me sweet and also to ensure I kept my mouth shut. I bought this house with the proceeds, it's not like I went on any extravagant holidays or anything. Please, you can't arrest me for this, you just can't."

"Did you carry out your duties under duress?" Sam asked. She liked this woman and was willing to give her the benefit of the doubt, providing she divulged what she knew about Phil Bradley's fake businesses.

"Sometimes, yes. I was very reluctant at first, until he dangled the carrot, and then... he hooked me. It didn't sit well with me ripping off those people, I swear it didn't. But I was desperate to buy my own house, and he used that to entice me into doing the unthinkable."

"Enticed you, or did he force you? Control you?"

"Yes, that's right. He controlled me. I did it the once, the adrenaline coursing through my veins, and then it was hard to stop. Maybe that's why he started touching me up, perhaps he saw me as his partner in crime and was keen to get more intimate. I never allowed it to get that far. God, I feel sick. I'm disgusted with myself. Now that I've revealed the truth, does that mean I will lose this house? Be put inside?" Her hands covered her face, and she sobbed.

Bob nudged Sam with his knee under the table. She glanced his way, and he rolled his eyes. He'd had enough. He couldn't stand it when he saw a perpetrator playing the victim. She winked at him, letting him know that all was in hand.

"Stop now. Tears don't wash with us, not in situations like this. You've already admitted you were in the wrong."

She sniffled and dabbed at her nose with a tissue from the box in the middle of the table. "I was but I also told you that he had control over me. It was like he had me hypnotised in a way."

"And you expect me to believe that?" Sam countered.

"I don't care what you believe, it's the truth. I got out of there as soon as I could."

"Once you'd gathered enough funds to buy this house," Bob interjected.

"Yes. No, that wasn't why at all. I've already told you, he touched me up, and I couldn't bear to be around him a moment longer."

"So the fact he was robbing innocent people of their savings didn't upset you in the slightest, it was only when he started touching you up that you wanted out of there. Jeez... you have some nerve, lady," Bob said, taking the lead once more.

Sam was happy to sit back and let him take over while she studied Dana's reaction. Dana swallowed, her gaze reverting back to the mug.

"What will happen to me now?" she whispered.

"It depends," Sam replied.

Dana's head rose, and her gaze latched on to Sam's. "On what?"

"On whether you're willing to work with us or not."

"I will. I promise, I'll do anything you want me to do, if it'll get me off the hook."

Sam wagged a finger. "Don't get me wrong, helping us with our enquiries won't necessarily get you off the hook, but it might lessen the charges the CPS are likely to throw at you."

"Lessen? Is that it? I spill the beans, give you everything you need to know about Phil, and you can't even guarantee that I'll get off with a lesser charge? Why should I help you?"

Sam leaned back and folded her arms. "I'm sorry, I sensed you had an ounce of remorse running through your body. I guess I was wrong." She unfolded her arms and went to stand.

Dana held up her hands. "Please, don't do this. I'm sorry, about everything. I should never have fallen under his spell. I will regret my decision to do anything underhand for the rest of my life. Why do you think I switched careers?"

"Very well. I'm going to need you to accompany me to the station, where we'll conduct an interview under caution."

"Yes, if it means you'll help me obtain a lesser charge, as promised."

"Let's get one thing straight, I didn't make any such promises. I definitely used the word *might* when I mentioned the CPS. Your fate is in their hands, not mine."

"I'm sorry, I didn't mean to presume. I'll do what I can to help."

"One more question before we leave," Sam said.

"Anything." Dana nodded enthusiastically.

"Were you aware that one of the fake businesses was set up in your name?"

"My God, no, I didn't know he'd done that. You have to believe me. I've been totally honest with you up until now. I wouldn't lie about this."

"Very well. Finish your drink, and we'll head back to the

183

station." Sam stood. "I won't be long, I need to make a call to pave the way for your arrival."

Sam left the kitchen and rang the station. "Nick, I've got someone I need to bring in for questioning under caution. Can you hold an interview room open for me?"

"Will do, ma'am. We'll expect to see you soon. I'll get everything set up for you now and arrange for one of my officers to sit in on the interview."

"Great. We'll be there within the next twenty minutes. Can you put me through to a member of my team now, please?"

"Doing it now."

The phone rang once before the ever-efficient Claire answered it.

"Claire, it's me. We've got some good news. We're bringing Dana Powell in for questioning. She's admitted that Phil Bradley started up several fake companies with the intention of getting people to invest their life savings."

"Wow, okay. What do you need from me, boss?"

"We've also visited the ex-wife, but we haven't got around to finding Jennifer Moriarty as yet. Can you ask a member of the team to find out what they know about this woman? I'm thinking there has to be a connection with Phil, judging by what we've encountered already today. Is there any way we can find out who the woman is who works alongside him at the office?"

"I'm sure I can make up some excuse to get that information... umm... if they're still open. Time is getting on."

"Don't let me hold you up. Ring me as soon as you find anything."

"I will." Claire was the one to hang up.

Sam paced the hallway for a few minutes, sensing that Claire would call her back ASAP. She wasn't disappointed.

"Boss, I just rang the office, and yes, Jennifer works there."

"Okay, and she's still at work, I take it... don't answer that, it's getting late in the day and my brain is in the process of shutting down. Ask Liam and Oliver to get over to Bradley's office, keep it under surveillance for now. We'll bring Dana Powell in and then shoot over there. I have a sense of urgency to bring Jennifer in now, as well."

"I'll get the boys organised. Give me a shout if I can do anything else for you."

Sam ended the call and returned to the kitchen. Bob and Dana both glanced her way.

"Another question, if I may? Jennifer Moriarty, what do you know about her?"

Dana shrugged. "The name doesn't sound familiar, so I would have to say, nothing, sorry."

"Okay. Let's go. Do you need to do anything before we leave?"

"No. I'm good, thanks."

Bob escorted Dana to the front door where all three of them put on their shoes. Then Bob put Dana in the back of Sam's car while she secured the front door.

THE DRIVE back to the station was carried out in silence, except for the one call Sam accepted from Liam in which he told her that he and Oliver were now stationed outside Bradley's office, awaiting further instructions.

Sam debated whether to dump Dana in a cell and to shoot over to the location or not but decided that wouldn't be fair on Dana who had so far been more than open with them about what had gone on behind closed doors at her former employer.

After careful consideration, she stuck to her original plan of questioning Dana under caution. The interview went without a hitch. Dana was open with them and full of remorse. She was arrested for fraud and deception and later released. Sam assured Dana, as she had assisted them with their enquiries, that she would bend over backwards to ensure CPS were aware of her cooperation and would treat her accordingly. Dana was sent home in a patrol car not long after the interview ended.

"Right, I think we should join Liam and Oliver. I'm going to sign out a Taser, just in case."

"In other words, your instinct is putting you on full alert and warning you to be cautious?"

"Correct. Let's hope this is our last call of the day."

"You're not alone there. I'm cream-crackered."

"Likewise."

THE TRAFFIC WAS bumper to bumper at that time of night, which only added to Sam's deteriorating mood. "Jesus, get moving, for fuck's sake. Why do people keep switching lanes at the drop of a hat? Both lanes are travelling at the same speed. Tossers!"

"My thoughts exactly. Idiots."

Sam ended up using her siren to get through the blockage which resulted in a few irate drivers blasting their horns and giving her the finger.

"Rude arseholes. They should be grateful we're in a hurry or I'd be hauling their arses in for abusing a police officer."

Bob laughed. "I love it when your anger emerges. You're priceless."

"I'm glad I amuse you. My job for the day is done."

A few streets away from their destination, Sam cut the siren and again ended up being ensnared in traffic. "I hate this town at this time of night, and these roadworks aren't helping much either."

"It's even worse going the other way out of town. I got

caught up for ten minutes last week at the three-way traffic lights. The cars before me all got fed up and did a U-turn to come back this way."

"Ha, I bet they regretted that decision."

Five minutes later, they pulled up behind Liam's car. Sam and Bob left their vehicle and jumped into the rear seats.

"Any good?" Sam asked.

"She's still in there," Liam said. "We keep seeing her go back and forth in the office, as though she's tidying up for the evening."

"What about Bradley, any sign of him inside?"

"Not seen him at all, not since we arrived, boss," Liam replied.

Just then the lights went out in the office and the front door opened. Jennifer Moriarty locked the front door and nipped around the back of the building, out of sight.

"Come on, Bob. Let's see what she's up to. Liam, get ready to follow us. She might be collecting a car or setting off on foot. Either way, we need to keep her on our radar."

Sam and Bob dashed back to their own vehicle and rounded the corner just in time to see a silver SUV pulling out of the car park behind Bradley's office.

"Hmm... okay, things are starting to add up now. Run the plate for me, Bob."

Bob contacted the station. Suzanna ran the licence number through the system, and it came back belonging to a red Merc. "Surprise, surprise, another fake plate. Thanks, Suzanna. We're on the killer's trail now. We've got Liam and Oliver with us for backup."

"Crikey. Glad you've got her in your sights. We'll await further news. Good luck."

"Thanks."

Sam deliberately kept her distance from the vehicle, which was a bit of a stretch at times, given the weather conditions and the amount of traffic still around. Jennifer appeared to speed up on the outskirts of town. Sam stayed with her until she blasted the car and sped off. In a panic, Sam pressed down hard on the accelerator but lost her.

She slammed her fist on the steering wheel. "Damn. What now?"

"We stick with it. Keep driving. She must have cottoned on to the fact we were following her. I'll check all the minor roads leading off, see if we can find her. Don't you dare get downhearted about this. She's here somewhere, all we've got to do is find her, simples."

Sam nodded, aware that her partner was right. She squeezed down hard on the accelerator and whizzed along the long stretch of road ahead of them.

"Stop, turn around. I saw a car with its lights on going up the country road on the left."

"Are you sure it was her?" Sam asked. She indicated and locked the steering wheel into position as she made the turn.

Liam did the same behind her to keep up. Sam indicated to go up the country lane, annoyed that the cars coming towards them refused to flash her, allowing her to cross their path.

"Bloody arseholes."

"Selfish bastards," Bob joined in the name-calling.

"What if it's not her? What if we're guilty of losing her and get called out to another murder scene tomorrow? I could never live with myself knowing that we had her in our grasp and let her go."

"Hey, I'm usually the negative one, not you. It'll come good, don't fret. Quick, go now before this one gets any closer."

Sam didn't hesitate. She turned into the lane to the sound of another horn being blasted. Bob raised two fingers to the driver and let out a couple more derogatory names.

"I can see the lights up ahead, there's a bend in the road. I'm going to hold back, keep my distance. Liam has managed to keep up with us."

"Great stuff. Keep your cool, and we'll nail her arse to the station wall before the night is out."

"I wish I had your faith, partner. Shit! I'm running out of petrol, I knew I should have topped up during the day."

"Seriously? You let it get that low? Are you crazy?"

"All right. I feel bad enough as it is without you having a go at me."

"Hopefully, her destination won't be too far up ahead. If I were you, I would turn off my lights."

"What? I could end up in a ditch or the hedge. Ain't gonna happen."

"Don't blame me if things go belly up, you've been warned."

Sam grunted and squinted at the road ahead, at the rear lights of the SUV. "She's still going. Hold on." She pressed down hard on the accelerator, and the car shot forward.

"Christ, I never knew you had it in you to tear down a country lane like this. You're risking her seeing you if you don't switch off your lights."

Sam cursed under her breath, switched off her lights and had to try and suppress the panic rising within as she continued to hurtle through the lane that was only slightly wider than her car. "On your head be it. I shouldn't have to remind you that this is a brand-new car."

"You'll thank me in the end, when we throw her arse in a cell."

The lights of the SUV disappeared up ahead.

"Has she turned off or come to a standstill and killed her engine?"

"Your guess is as good as mine."

She decided it would be best to slow down until they

could assess the situation once they were out in the open up ahead. She also had the reassurance that Liam had managed to catch her up and was right behind her.

Sam approached the bend in the road to find the yard of a farm right ahead of her. It was lit by floodlights. Two cars, one being the SUV and an older car, sat in the drive alongside a tractor and an old Land Rover. There were three lights on downstairs in the house. Sam could see two people, a man and a woman, having a conversation in front of the window in the kitchen.

She pointed them out to Bob. "Can you make out who they are?"

"We're too far. We're going to need to get closer."

Liam drew up beside her. Sam was pleased to see that he, too, had driven through the lane without his lights on.

"We'll get out of the car quietly and have a word with the others."

Once they were in the back of Liam's car, a plan formulated in Sam's mind. "Do we know who owns this place?"

Oliver was on his phone. "White Oak Farm belongs to a Mr John Palmer. The farm has been in the family for decades. They're renowned cattle farmers in the area, as well as making and selling superb cheese and ice cream far and wide."

"A thriving business and another victim in the making. We need to do all we can to prevent that from happening. Oliver, while you have your phone out, ring Claire, check out the other car for me. We don't know what car Bradley drives, or do we?"

"I don't think so, boss."

Oliver rang the incident room, and Claire gave them the information within a few seconds, which corroborated what they thought. The two vehicles on site belonged to Bradley, and who would appear to be his accomplice in the murders, Jennifer Moriarty.

"Okay, now we've been armed with the facts, it's time to make our move."

Bob reached for his phone. "Want me to call for backup? An armed response team?"

"I'd rather not. I think we're more than capable of restraining the suspects ourselves. Does anyone here think differently?"

"I'm up for it," Liam replied.

"So am I," Oliver added.

Sam's gaze drifted to her partner. Their eyes met in the dark, and he sighed.

"Okay. On your head be it. What's the plan?"

"We obviously need to get in there, and quickly. I think, Bob, you and Liam should take the back, while Oliver and I approach the front door as if nothing has happened. I'm armed with my Taser, should it be needed. Have you guys got your sprays and batons to hand?"

"Check," her three colleagues replied in unison.

"Good. You know what to do, Bob, get in through the back way as soon as you can. You should be able to hear the doorbell ringing. Take your cue from that. Break a window to gain entry if you have to. We need to get in there before it's too late for Palmer." Sam shrugged. "Hopefully it's not too late already. Everyone understand? Any questions?"

"I have plenty," Bob muttered, "but they'll keep."

Sam punched him in the thigh. "I'm being serious. We have a man and possibly his whole family at risk in there, and you're out here playing the fool."

"Sorry. I wasn't, not really. I do have genuine doubts if we're doing the right thing going in there without backup, armed backup, in place."

Sam shook her head and exhaled a frustrated breath. "I fear time isn't on our side. Which is why we need to make our move now. We've got this, guys. Work swiftly and efficiently to disarm the perpetrators and secure the safety of Palmer and his family, if he has one. Don't put yourselves in unnecessary danger, remain in pairs to get the job done. Is that clear? Are we ready?"

Sam raised her clenched fist, and the others rammed theirs against hers.

"Let's do this. Ensure your phones are on silent before we set off. Right, let's go. Don't forget, don't make a move out the back until we've rung the doorbell. We'll give you a chance to get into position first before we make our move. Good luck, Bob and Liam. No unnecessary bravery, you hear me. In and out, no lingering. We'll call for backup once we've secured the safety of Palmer and his family."

They set off and split up at the side elevation of the farmhouse. Sam and Oliver stayed in position for a few extra seconds and then moved to the front of the property.

Sam checked her Taser was tucked into the waistband of her trousers before she rang the bell. "Are you okay?"

Oliver gave a brief nod and peered through the window on his right. "I can see a man sitting upright in a dining chair in the front room. Looks like he's tied up."

The next second the front door opened, and Jennifer Moriarty was standing there. Sam flashed her ID in the woman's face. The door began to close, but Oliver shoulder-charged it and sent the woman tumbling to the floor. The large knife she'd been holding scuttled across the Minton-tiled hallway. Oliver pounced on it with his gloved hands. Jennifer got to her feet and screamed at him. Sam produced her Taser, anxiously glancing around her to see where Bradley was. Bob and Liam entered the hallway at the other end. As soon as she laid eyes on the rest of the team, Jennifer screamed again, dipped her head and ran at Bob. Her head connected with his midriff, and he let out a grunt. Jennifer stood upright and dashed towards the back door.

"Don't let her get away, Liam. Use force if necessary. Bob, ring for backup."

Her partner clenched his stomach and stared at her.

Sam refused to get into an argument with him and, with Oliver behind her, went in search of Bradley. With her Taser drawn, she entered the front room where Oliver had seen the man tied to the chair. The man was still there, he had gaffer tape over his mouth, but his eyes were panic stricken and kept darting to the wall beside her. She peered around the door, and there, standing behind it, was Phil Bradley, holding a gun to Sam's chest.

"We appear to be at an impasse, Mr Bradley. Drop your weapon or I'll shoot."

Bradley's gaze flitted behind Sam and to the right, where the victim was sitting.

"Don't even think about it." If Oliver had been armed, she wouldn't have had any hesitation in asking him to protect Palmer, but he wasn't. A baton and pepper spray weren't going to cut it in this situation.

"Are you all right, Mr Palmer?" Sam asked.

The man, his eyes widened in fear, nodded and gave a muffled, indecipherable reply.

"Good. We'll have you out of your confines soon enough, bear with us." Sam turned her attention back to Bradley. "Stop being foolish and surrender, Bradley. We've got all the evidence we need to close this case. Drop your weapon and make this easier on yourself."

"I didn't do it... kill them. I only killed the first one, Tammy. The others were down to Jen, she's the one you need to arrest for the other murders. I told her not to do it. Said carrying out the murders too soon would invite your lot to snoop around."

"You were right. You both left an unnecessary trail that led us back to you without much effort on our part. Give it up now, while you can. This place is about to be flooded with armed police. You know what their motto is, 'shoot first, ask questions later.'" It wasn't, but it was all Sam could come up with at a moment's notice to make him rethink his actions. The misinformation appeared to work for an instant, judging by the confusion Sam spotted on his face.

He dithered for a second or two, took a step towards her, then retreated again. Stepped to his right only to return a few nanoseconds later. The uncertainty grew in his eyes until Sam took a chance and moved closer to him.

Bradley waved the gun at her. "Come any closer and I'll shoot."

Sam raised her free hand. "Everything is cool. Drop your weapon, and we can discuss your theory behind the murders down at the station."

"You're not taking me in. I'm not going down for this, I refuse to. Back away or I'll shoot, that's your last warning, bitch."

"Come now, don't be foolish. If what you told me was true, that you're only responsible for one murder, you won't go down for long, but your confession could help us throw the book at Jennifer. All this was her doing, wasn't it?"

Bradley stared at Sam, frantic, like a deer caught in the headlights, and nodded.

"What changed?"

"She joined the firm. It didn't take her long to realise what I was up to. She's an intelligent woman but she has an evil streak. She came up with the idea of revisiting the people I had conned out of the money to get the rest of their savings out of them, aware that no one ties up all their money in stocks and shares. I told her she was being greedy and that it would end badly. She laughed at me, told me I was right because the victims would need to be killed."

"If you were against it, why go through with it?"

He fell silent. Sam could tell he was digging deep for an answer. "She had me over a barrel."

Sam inclined her head. "How?" She thought hard, and she remembered what Dana had told her about him having wandering hands in the office and hit him with it. "You made the mistake of touching up the wrong person, didn't you?"

He stared at her long and hard and then nodded. "Yes. All I wanted—no, needed—was a bit of female company. Why did Dana have to leave me? She understood me fully, until…"

"You laid a hand on her. There's a difference between women being friendly towards you and inviting you to grope them. No woman appreciates that kind of attention."

"You think? I have doubts about the truth behind such a comment."

"I'm telling you, it's the truth. Women have a right to be treated as equals to their male colleagues. Just because you work closely with someone, it doesn't give you the authority to touch them up."

Palmer groaned and wiggled in his chair to gain their attention. Without removing her gaze from Bradley, she said, "It's all right, Mr Palmer, you'll be set free soon, you have my word."

The hostage calmed down, allowing Sam to get back to her discussion with Bradley. "Come on, Phil. Why don't you just admit all of this has been a huge mistake and move on?"

Footsteps sounded in the hallway behind her. "We've got her. She's told us that the murders were all Bradley's idea," Bob shouted.

"They weren't. I've told you the truth. She's a liar. Passing the buck to save her own skin. I refuse to allow that to happen." His hand wavered, his temper growing.

Sam felt he was becoming unstable before her eyes and that he was liable to do something dangerous if she pushed him further. "I believe you. You and me, Phil, we can work together, make sure the jury are aware of the truth. We can't allow her to get away with this, can we?"

"No. We can't allow it. She's a manipulative bitch. I refuse to go down with her. I didn't have these thoughts until I met her. All this is her fault. She's responsible for all the murders. We would have killed him, too, if you hadn't shown up."

Palmer shouted something behind the tape and his chair moved violently on the spot.

"It's all right, Mr Palmer. You're safe now. I won't allow anything to happen to you. You won't either, will you, Phil?"

Phil's gaze flitted over to where Palmer was tied up. "I never wanted it to go this far."

"It started off by you using the money to pay off your gambling debts, didn't it?" Sam asked.

"How do you know about that?"

"We spoke to your ex-wife."

He shook his head. "I loved her; she betrayed me. Kicked me out when I was at my lowest ebb. I toyed with the idea of killing her but I couldn't bring myself to do it because, deep down, I still love her. I tried to get back with her; she was having none of it. As soon as I signed over the house, she didn't want to know. Selling that house, taking the fifty-fifty would have solved a few, not all, of my problems. Paid off a number of my debts, but she managed to talk me around. She always did have me wrapped around her finger."

His hand dropped a little. Sam pressed her finger on the trigger, sensing that her opportunity to strike was only seconds away.

However, at the last minute, Bradley regained his composure, and the anger blazed in his eyes once more.

"Phil, let's talk about this some more down at the station."

His head slowly moved from one side to the other. "No, it's too late. She's already done the damage, pointed the finger at me. When it comes to the crunch, the jury always side with you women, don't they?"

"Not every time. If you can win them over, like you have me, then all is not lost. We need to prove that Jennifer manipulated you and forced you to go along with the plan you've spoken about."

"They won't listen to me. They'll take one look at her beautiful face, and she's bound to turn on the tears, and that will be my undoing, won't it?"

"Not necessarily. Not if you give us a statement, a confession under caution. That will work in your favour, I promise you. We have enough evidence to throw the book at her, but you're going to need to give us the ins and outs of what actually went on behind the scenes."

That way, you're bound to give us enough information about your involvement, too, enough to bang you up for life!

"You'd be willing to do that? Work with me? Even after me killing Tammy Callard?"

"Of course. We'll tell the court it was under duress, that Jennifer was the brains behind the crimes. That you never had a killer instinct until she breezed into your life. That's true, isn't it?"

"Yes. She took advantage of my good nature. Blackmailed me into going after the victims like I've told you already. Why? Why did I listen to her? All of this could have been avoided. None of this should have happened. Those three people needn't have died. At the end of the day, who is really to blame for their demise? Me. I am. I can blame Jennifer for going so far but I was the one who allowed it to happen when I could have prevented three needless murders. I'm to blame, no one else."

"You're wrong. You were vulnerable, down on your luck,

fed up with life. She used that to manipulate you. What was her recompense for the murders? Did she take a cut of the money?"

"Yes, every time."

"There you are then. How could all this be your fault?"

He closed his eyes, and for an instant, Sam contemplated firing her Taser. The day was catching up on her. She could take him out and then book him and Jennifer into a cell for the night and go home, leave them to consider their failings overnight and tackle them both during the interviews in the morning.

Bradley's eyes flew open. He stared at her, and suddenly something shifted in his demeanour that made her nervous. The gun slowly turned towards his head. Sam took the shot before he had the chance to release a bullet in his temple. Bradley crumpled to the floor, fifty thousand volts shooting through him.

Oliver and Bob jumped into action. Bob had his cuffs at the ready, standing over Bradley who had dropped his weapon. Oliver picked it up and disarmed it before he placed it in an evidence bag. Sam released her finger, allowing Bob to cuff Bradley. He was still stunned by the encounter. The tears of frustration emerged and ran down his cheeks. Bob yanked Bradley to his feet and marched him past Sam.

"Wait, I have a few words I want to say to him first. You can forget everything I said about working with you. We have all the evidence we need on both of you, to send you down for life. It would make my skin crawl to work with you, a man willing to take innocent lives just to pay off his debts. You're despicable. Get him out of my sight, Sergeant. I'll deal with him back at the station."

"But you promised," Phil whined.

"Shut up. She owes you nothing," Bob shouted in Bradley's ear and forced him out to the awaiting car.

Between them, Oliver and Sam released Mr Palmer.

He sobbed with relief the second his hands were set free. "Thank you. If you hadn't come along, I dread to think what would have happened to me."

"You're safe now, that's all that matters. Is there anyone else in the house?"

"No. I live alone, my wife died last year. That's how I met Bradley. I wanted to invest what she left me, tie it up, ready for my retirement. I had no idea he was dodgy or that I would end up with my life hanging by a thread."

Sam squeezed his shoulder. "We're going to ring for an ambulance, get you checked over."

"I'm fine. Don't waste their time."

"I can't leave you like this. Is there a friend or relative we can call to come and be with you?"

"My neighbour. I'll ring him now. You go, I'll be fine. Wait, you'll be wanting a statement from me, won't you?"

"Don't worry about that for now. In the next few days will do. Are you sure you'll be all right?"

"I'm sure. And, Inspector?"

"Yes, sir?"

"Thank you for saving my life."

"You don't have to thank us, we were just doing our job. Glad it was a happy ending this time around."

"Believe me, so am I. Thanks again."

Sam smiled and patted him on the forearm. "You're welcome."

She left the house with Oliver in time to see the backup teams arriving. She ran through what needed to be done and asked a female officer to take down Mr Palmer's statement, if he was up to it. Then she and her team drove back to the station with the two prisoners.

Jennifer Moriarty kicked up a major fuss when she was transferred from the back of Liam's car but, in contrast,

Bradley accompanied them without complaint. In fact, he didn't utter a word until they reached the custody suite. Sam had ensured the couple didn't meet en route, which seemed to appease Bradley.

Sam made sure the prisoners were tucked up in their cells before she headed back to the incident room to congratulate her team on a job well done.

"Go home, peeps. We'll deal with the paperwork and the interviews in the morning. You never cease to amaze me, all of you. That's another successful case wrapped up."

EPILOGUE

*S*am arrived home that evening dead on her feet, mentally and physically tired after bringing the case to a satisfactory conclusion. Rhys wasn't home yet. She rang him while she was still in the car. "Hi, it's me. Are you going to be long?"

"I'm five minutes away. Sorry, I should have called you. Have you been home long?"

"No, I've only just pulled up myself. I'll nip and get Sonny, take him for a walk, unless you want to come with us?"

"I'll leave it for tonight. I've got a surprise for you, but it'll keep until later."

"You tease. Okay. See you soon."

Sam left the car and collected Sonny from Doreen's. "How has he been today?"

"All good. Oh dear, you look shattered, love. Come in, his walk can wait, let me make you a cuppa."

Sam smiled. "As inviting as that sounds, Doreen, I have to go for a walk to clear my head, if you don't mind?"

"Not at all. You carry on. What about dinner? I have some

leftover stew you're welcome to have, there's enough for both of you."

"Honestly, we're fine. Stick it in the freezer for yourself for a meal for next week."

Doreen chuckled. "That's a great idea. Enjoy your walk. Take care, Sam."

Sonny tugged on the lead, anxious to get to the park. Sam let him off and tipped back her head to expel the stale air settled in her lungs and renewed it with the fresh air surrounding her.

Sonny bounded around the park, going up to visit his four-legged friends and then coming back to her once he'd said hello.

"Come on, you, enough for today. Let's get home and start on the dinner, whatever that might be."

Sonny whimpered and sat while she attached his lead. When she glanced up, she saw Rhys coming towards her. She had trouble making out what he was carrying in the dark. She was none the wiser when he stopped a few feet in front of them.

"Hello, you. What have you got there?"

Rhys smiled and got down on one knee. *Oh God, he's going to propose!*

"What's going on?" Sam asked, her nerves making her voice tremble.

Rhys placed a finger to his lips and opened his jacket. A tiny head popped out, and Sam's heart melted in an instant. She took a few steps closer and crouched in front of him. She hooked an arm over Sonny's back as he sniffed the pup.

"My God. You never said you were getting another dog. Boy or girl?"

"Another boy. He's a Labrador."

"He's absolutely adorable. Does he have a name?"

"Not yet. I thought we could figure that out together."

Sam held out her arms for a cuddle. "Welcome to the family, little one. You'll want for nothing with us, your big brother will tell you as much." Tears dripped onto her cheeks, and she snuggled her face into his soft fur.

Rhys wiped her tears away. "Don't, you'll start me off. Here's to new beginnings, for all of us."

Sonny whimpered and licked the pup on the nose.

Sam laughed. "I think his big brother approves of the new addition."

THE END

THANK you for reading To Control Them the next thrilling adventure **To Endanger Lives** is now available.

HAVE you read any of my fast paced other crime thrillers yet? Why not try the first book in the DI Sara Ramsey series No Right to Kill

OR GRAB the first book in the bestselling, award-winning, Justice series here, Cruel Justice.

OR THE FIRST book in the spin-off Justice Again series, Gone In Seconds.

.   .   .

PERHAPS YOU'D PREFER to try one of my other police procedural series, the DI Kayli Bright series which begins with The Missing Children.

OR MAYBE YOU'D enjoy the DI Sally Parker series set in Norfolk, Wrong Place.

OR MY GRITTY police procedural starring DI Nelson set in Manchester, Torn Apart.

OR MAYBE YOU'D like to try one of my successful psychological thrillers She's Gone, I KNOW THE TRUTH or Shattered Lives.

KEEP IN TOUCH WITH M A COMLEY

Pick up a FREE novella by signing up to my newsletter today.
https://BookHip.com/WBRTGW

BookBub
www.bookbub.com/authors/m-a-comley

Blog

http://melcomley.blogspot.com

Why not join my special Facebook group to take part in monthly giveaways.

Readers' Group

Printed in Great Britain
by Amazon

21582921R00129